LI[illegible]ES

BY

ANN LINGARD

Knowledge Exchange Fellow
at the Centre for Cognitive Ageing and
Cognitive Epidemiology,
Department of Psychology, University of Edinburgh

With a foreword by
Professor Ian Deary

www.lbclifetimes.org

First published in the United Kingdom in 2014
by
The University of Edinburgh Centre for Cognitive Ageing
and Cognitive Epidemiology

THE UNIVERSITY
of EDINBURGH

Centre for Cognitive Ageing
and Cognitive Epidemiology

www.ccace.ed.ac.uk

CCACE is funded by the
Lifelong Health and Wellbeing Initiative

Lifelong Health
& Wellbeing
Research for Healthy Ageing

www.mrc.ac.uk/LLHW

ISBN 978-0-9928884-0-4

Cover design by Edinburgh Printing Services
Cover Image: © iStockphoto

LBC LIFETIMES

1. Introduction, by Ian Deary

Ian Deary talking about the 1936 mental health survey

Writing this introduction finds me in an unusual area. I am used to directing a team of researchers, and I am used to analysing data and preparing research reports for scientific journals. However, the interest that the Lothian Birth Cohorts have attracted from artists of different disciplines has surprised me. So, apart from the papers we have produced in scientific journals, I have seen a wider range of products from the research: video/photographic exhibitions, an Edinburgh Festival fringe play, and a series of portraits. And now this series of 'brief lives'. Not just that, but the lives of both the participants and the researchers are described. Usually, we researchers manage to stay in the background and avoid being the focus of attention. It's made me think about why this has come about.

Starting the Lothian Birth Cohort Studies of 1921 and 1936 was an easy decision in principle, though harder to bring about in practice (because funding longitudinal studies of larger numbers of people is expensive). When it was discovered that there were childhood cognitive test scores for almost all Scottish people born in 1921 and 1936, it was immediately obvious that these individuals could form the basis of an invaluable research programme into human cognitive ageing.

That is, they could uniquely tell us about why some people—across the life course—age better than others with respect to their brain and mental capabilities. Therefore, from 1999 onwards we sought permission to re-contact some of the Lothian-resident people who had taken the mental survey test in 1932 or 1947 and follow them up in old age. To date, we have seen the Lothian Birth Cohort 1921 at age 79, 83, 87, 90, and 92. They are currently—and likely to remain—the longest follow-up study of human cognition in the world. We have seen the younger Lothian Birth Cohort at age 70, 73, and 76. Neither study is complete; we are still following them up. And they do a great deal for us when our research team sees them—about once every three years. They undertake a long battery (yes, that's the official name for it) of cognitive and medical tests, they provide several blood samples, they take a brain scan, and they complete a long series of questionnaires. We have gathered a huge amount of information about their bodies, brains, and lifestyles. These data have led to many high-profile scientific publications (see http://www.lothianbirthcohort.ed.ac.uk); indeed, the cohorts have become famous around the scientific world for their important and sometimes unique contributions to the science of cognitive and brain ageing.

Even with all the data we collect from them, one realises that something of the person can be missing. We are typically publishing results that find relationships among hundreds of people rather than something that applies to an individual. That's important. In science, larger studies mean more precise results. But the large residue of these generalities is each person's uniqueness. Therefore, it is a pleasure to see Ann Lingard's celebration of the Lothian Birth Cohorts' individuality. It is a shame that we couldn't include everyone.

It's a pleasure, on the other hand, to see some of my fellow scientists described and celebrated too. So, this is a thank you to Ann for her interest, warm thanks to the Lothian Birth Cohorts for their dedication to and persistence with the studies, and thanks to the research team whose enthusiasm and excellence provide the scientific outputs and international recognition that the cohorts deserve.

The Lothian Birth Cohorts have good friends, and they have grown beyond their origins. On friends, Age UK has supported the Lothian Birth Cohort since it started. Our scientific team has a good, close, and long-lasting relationship with them. We share a knowledge exchange plan with Age UK; that is, we work together to broadcast the results beyond the scientific journals. On growth, the Lothian Birth Cohorts can take a lot of the credit for bringing about the Centre for Cognitive Ageing and Cognitive Epidemiology (CCACE) at the University of Edinburgh. This is funded by the UK's Research Councils (especially the Medical Research Council and the Biotechnology and Biological Sciences Research Council) under their 'Life Long Health and Wellbeing' programme. CCACE started in 2008 and is funded until 2018 after a successful application for renewal in 2013. One of CCACE's aims is "to elucidate the routes to the vulnerable ageing brain"; the Lothian Birth Cohorts are the Centre's flagship projects in doing so. Thanks go to Age UK, CCACE and the University of Edinburgh School of Philosophy, Psychology and Language Sciences for supporting the publication of this book.

Professor Ian Deary, January 2014
Director, The University of Edinburgh Centre for Cognitive Ageing and Cognitive Epidemiology   www.ccace.ed.ac.uk

2. Ann Lingard

Ann Lingard lives on a small-holding at the edge of the Lake District and within sight of the Scottish coast, and rears Herdwick sheep. Formerly a research scientist and academic at Cambridge and Glasgow universities, she is now a writer and broadcaster.

Ann with sheep and dog

As well as her published novels, short stories and many factual articles, Ann continues to write the series of *Solway Shore Stories,* during which she has met and talked to people who live and work along the coast of the Solway Firth.
As a 'Bright Ideas' Visiting Fellow at the ESRC Genomics Forum in Edinburgh she researched and wrote the human stories of some of the exhibits in the Surgeons' Hall Museum, as well as meeting and writing about people involved in the present-day tissue and blood donation process.

These *LBC Lifetimes* are the results of meeting several of the people involved in the Lothian Birth Cohort studies, not only members of the LBC1921 and LBC1936 cohorts but also members of the research team, and listening to and recording their life-stories.

www.annlingard.com
www.solwayshorestories.co.uk

3. Writing the stories

'How do you try to find the 'essence' of a person?'
That was the question I asked myself, in the face of the wealth of medical and cognitive information that has been collected about each person taking part in the Cognitive Ageing project.
I hoped that I could find an answer for at least some of the participants by listening to them – the 'story-givers' – and writing their stories.

When Ian Deary and Robin Morton asked me to write about some of these participants in the Lothian Birth Cohort studies and some of the people who collected and analysed their cognitive data, I was handed a dream project – meeting people of all ages and backgrounds and hearing about their lives, finding out about the science and ideas underlying the Cohort studies, and also spending time in Edinburgh. And indeed it turned out to be a fascinating and inspiring year for me, a year of listening, questioning, and writing.

I especially want to thank the LBC story-tellers for all their kindness. They invited me into their homes, and were so generous with their time and trust: they have shown me photos and objects that were dear to them, some of them have expounded their philosophies or political views, and they've told me touching, or sad or hilarious stories. I have been enchanted by their humour – the laughter, the exclamations, the self-deprecatory but joking remarks ...! I was surprised (but should not have been) at the diversity of their lives and backgrounds, and I learnt a great deal about Comptometer machines, 'counted cross-stitch', and why you should never grab the bottom of a rope dangling from a

rescue helicopter.
In all cases I came away from our meetings not only with a smile on my face, but also feeling very privileged to have shared in the stories of their lifetimes.

Everyone who has told me his or her story has shown that *'what is truly important'* is very different for each individual person.
For me, this has been a moving and thought-provoking experience, and always inspiring. I hope I have been able to capture each individual 'voice' from my copious notes, and to do their stories justice.

I also 'shadowed' one of the 1936 Cohort volunteers, Eddie Dishon, through his test sessions and was impressed at the range of tests he participated in, not least because of the length of the session and the concentration required. My own scientific training was not in psychology, so it has been interesting for me to learn about the rationale behind the various tests, as well as about the techniques for imaging and assessing all the data.

But, stories aside, the main characteristic that unites this extraordinary group of LBC volunteers, all in their seventies and nineties, and which has so impressed the research team and me, is their continued willingness to keep active, physically and mentally – and to *get involved*, whether in gardening, teaching others to sew, putting on fund-raising shows or, above all, in the cohort studies to which they keep coming back. Many of them also share a delightful pragmatism and great sense of humour.

I'm indebted to Professor Ian Deary, and Age UK and the

University of Edinburgh's Knowledge Exchange Fellowship scheme, for inviting and supporting my involvement in the Cohort studies. My thanks also go to Dave Liewald at CCACE for designing and setting up the *Lifetimes* website, www.lbclifetimes.org (where there are many more images relating to each story), and to Dr Robin Morton for all his help in facilitating the project.

A final note: every story-teller read the first draft of his or her story, and made any corrections or deletions they wished (there were very few); all LBC participants were given the opportunity to use a fictional name (only one did so and later changed her mind).

Ann Lingard, January 2014

The Lifetimes

Ronald Anderson	LBC1921
Helen Lamb	LBC1936
Alison Pattie	Cognitive Ageing team, CCACE
Thomas Young	LBC1936
Mark Bastin	Western General Infirmary
Margaret McKie	LBC1921
Maisie Brown	LBC1936
Donald Lyall	Cognitive Ageing team, CCACE
Eddie Dishon	LBC1936
Ian Deary	Director, CCACE
Elspeth Dougall	LBC1936

Ronald Anderson

LBC1921

Joinery?
"Oh yes, I can do that too!"
Mr Anderson's laugh, like his voice, is quiet. He tells me that he has made furniture, even a cabinet for a radiogram. "I still have cupboards of tools," he says, "But I'm a bit short on energy these days."
The wood for that furniture and for wood-turning on his lathe came from an unusual source: "I used to go to the ship-breaking yards at Bo'ness – we were able to get old wooden fittings from the breaking-up. I got some lovely old wood – teaks, mahogany – you couldn't buy it now."

The house where he and his wife Moira have lived since 1977, in Traquair Park West, is a red sandstone terraced house; sunlight is flooding into the room and picking out the decorative plaster cornicing and the Mother's Day cards on the mantel-piece, and we have been talking about panelled wooden doors and fine Victorian craftsmanship. Mrs Anderson has brought in a tray of tea and biscuits, and stays for a few minutes to talk about the house. She tells me it "was in a terrible state," when they bought it, "and the decoration was awful. One room had a dark green ceiling, another was dark brown!" Ah yes – the 'seventies, and all those striking 'contrast' colours... "Keeping the house in order kept me busy," her husband adds.

The overgrown garden needed a lot of attention too: there is a small garden with a low wall at the front, but at the back it is quite extensive. Mr Anderson used to grow vegetables, and tomatoes in the greenhouse, but he and his wife now prefer to grow flowers (a packet of Thomson & Morgan plant-plugs has just been delivered when I arrive)and he tells me, "Moira is the one who does the gardening now, she does the good half of it."

But building, renovating and repairing things seem to have been an important part of his life, outside his work. When he was a young man, he built his own television set in time for the Coronation. "I adapted ex-government equipment. It only had a six-inch screen! It was just a little box, but we had all the neighbours in to watch." Self-taught, he had built one of the very early radios, a crystal-set with headphones and a long outside aerial; there was only one station, but very good reception. Other radios followed, including that for the radiogram but, "once valves went, I stopped." Later he always did the car repairs, too, because "the boys always needed things done on theirs."

Mr Anderson, white-haired, spectacled, wearing a beige V-necked pullover over his shirt and trousers, sits in an armchair that is shaded from the sun, and speaks quietly, with modest reticence, about his early life. "We lived away out in the back of beyond for many years, near Bathgate. My father was a water engineer." A simple statement, but gradually it becomes clear that his father supervised the water supply for a unique and extraordinary community, at Bangour Village Hospital near Dechmont.

The hospital was opened in 1906 as a psychiatric hospital, although it was requisitioned as a military hospital during both World Wars. Unlike most hospitals, though, it comprised a small 'village' of about thirty separate villas of varying styles and sizes, in addition to the main hospital building itself.

The Anderson's cottage in the Bangour grounds

"It was a sort of community and we were all part of it, I suppose you could say it was almost a family event. All the workers were treated as part of the family. Everything was in its place, it was self-contained – each house had its own kitchen, and there were separate wards."

The Andersons had a cottage in the grounds, because Mr Anderson's father supervised the maintenance of the reservoir and the water-filtration system for the community. "We were completely self-contained – there was a farm at the hospital too, with a herd of dairy cows, and they grew their own grain on the farm, and oats and silage." Bangour also had its own tailoring shop, woodwork shop and joinery. "It even had its own railway station. Bangour was quite unique, it's worth a story on its own. It was all quite remote."

Self-sufficiency was part of family life: "I grew up with it. My father was always keen on growing vegetables though it was difficult because we were up at seven-to-eight hundred feet, in the snowier belt." Did they keep hens? "No, but we had turkeys – they were our friends. Everyone used to laugh at that." His eyes glimmer with quiet amusement.

The turkey 'friends'

"We'd grow them on and we'd sell them at Christmas. We never ate them, I wouldn't even eat chicken until five years ago."
Mr Anderson had three sisters – "I was by far the youngest" – and they were self-sufficient in their play, too: "We had our own method of playing – we invented our own games." And there was plenty for the adults, "concerts, a cinema, dances for the staff – everybody knew everybody else."

When he reached school age, he walked the 1½ miles to and from the local primary school each day. Secondary school, where he sat the Moray House intelligence test, was at Bathgate, a 1½-mile walk to the main road, then a bus to Bathgate Academy. "I never thought anything of it. I'd set off in the morning and walk back at night. Sometimes folks would be horrified, they'd ask me 'What if you met a mental patient?'." But the patients didn't frighten him, he says – some of them were even given paid employment, as tailors for example.

He left school in 1938, aged seventeen, and got a job as a road surveyor for the council in Linlithgow, cycling "over the hills" to get there. In 1942, his training took him into the Royal Artillery School of Surveying, after which he returned to the family home at Bangour; he was still living at home in 1947. Then his father retired so, because the cottage was tied to the job, they all moved to Linlithgow for a couple of years, and from there to Broxburn, which was then still the hub of the shale industry.

He continued as a surveyor, staying with the Local Authorities, but moving from Lothian region to Edinburgh. "I came to the big city! The move to Edinburgh was a big change from the rural environment, and I had quite serious thoughts about it. But I was the only one that escaped – my sisters never married."

Moira too worked for the Highways Department, and it was here that she and Ronald Anderson met. "I was quite late marrying, not until 1961," he tells me, again with that quiet smile. They moved into a house opposite the zoo, and it was during this period that their daughter and two sons were born. The daughter has remained in Edinburgh, but the sons live in Sussex and Oxfordshire: despite this, they still see a lot of each other and their five grandchildren and, from earlier remarks during our conversation about the house, Mrs Anderson clearly enjoys having the rooms full of family.

Mr Anderson moved upwards through the Highway Department to become its Assistant Director; he oversaw the building of roads in Livingston New Town – "It was all open fields when we started" – and the final large scheme he supervised before retirement was the City by-pass. The job had its own special challenges, "two phases" as he calls it, because not only did he have to arrange and supervise the work of his own staff, such as the engineers, but he also had to work closely with Edinburgh City Council. "That side was totally different. I had to keep the two phases quite separate – we couldn't give in totally to the council, but we were managing and producing programmes for them to approve and finance." Meetings with the Highways Committee required him always to give explanations and reasons, frustrating for a man who clearly prefers to get on and do things.

After he retired in 1986, he and Moira "did a Far East tour.

We spent a month or so visiting Singapore, Hong Kong, then Bangkok, and went on to Bali. Moira is very keen on travel so I have to go along" (again that glimmering smile). "We used to have a caravan, and we toured it all round Europe, mainly in the Mediterranean region – the children loved it, they used to tumble out of the car whenever we arrived." Although they no longer have the caravan, he and Moira would drive to Caravan Club meets all around the local area. "The meets were very sociable. Moira especially enjoyed the Saturday dances – we're both very keen on ballroom and country dancing." Last year their Golden Wedding anniversary and his ninetieth birthday coincided, so they held a big 'get-together' for their family and friends at a favourite restaurant in Bathgate Country Park.

He still finds it "a little bit of a mystery how [he] got involved" with the Cohort Study, but he is enjoying the participation. "I look forward to hearing the results especially if they're good results. Nothing's deteriorated as much as I'd expected!" He went to one of the Cohort reunions, and "as the names of the schools were called out we had to stand up, but there were only three of us from Bathgate and we didn't really know each other."

Just before I leave I wonder if there is anything he regrets he hasn't had time to do, and another quiet statement brings a surprise. "I would have liked to visit Australia and South America, I've been to most other places."
Such as Africa: in the 1980s, he says, "I had two four-month spells in Africa after I retired, in Botswana to set up a civil engineering training school. I had to set it up from scratch. It was a whole new venture – I got into the way of black folks' thinking, it was quite amusing. And I did a fair bit of lecturing

as well." The training school was tied to the University. "Usually the students would go to sleep – I had to be very careful not to overstep. And to understand their ways of working. They'd be out at night drinking and this was when they'd catch up on their sleep!"

"It was as much about educating the staff and local government officers on the necessity of engineering training. About a third of them were very keen, and very clever, they could see a future in it. They're very progressive in Botswana."

How did he get the job? "The Reader's Digest had an advertisement for a government mission to set up the school and to educate the students." He applied, and now he laughs as he says, "To my horror I was asked to go out there! There was no salary, but they paid for my hotel and travel – and for Moira to come out and visit too. They were very nice people, I enjoyed working with them. And when Moira came out [for a month on each tour] she helped with the clerical side."

"I'm quite sure that growing up in Bangour coloured my life for the whole future – I felt the importance of community and individual lives"

March 2012

Helen Lamb

LBC1936

"Grandpa had a poultry farm out at Bathgate. He'd come in an old car to collect me Friday lunch-time – it had plastic window-things that flapped – and I'd go to stay with them the whole summer. I loved it there, I ran wild like a gypsy."

The farm was certainly different from where Helen Lamb grew up, in a house in the Carrick Knowe area of Edinburgh – although she was able to 'run wild' there too.
Her grandparents' house had no electricity or running water. "There were paraffin lamps, and a toilet – we called it a shunkie, I think that's probably a rude word! – way out the back. Granny cooked on the fire. There was a bed recess in the living room with a curtain where my grandparents slept, and I had to sleep in a wee room at the back, it was freezing cold."
"There was a big wooden hut with the chicks in incubators, hundreds of them, with the lights above to keep them warm." The chicks grew up, of course: "I must have been sadistic as a child," Helen laughs as she speaks. "I'd watch Grandpa wring their necks, I can still remember how they'd keep twitching as he carried them up the field ... Granny would sit on the corner bench outside, and I can still see her, knee-deep in feathers, plucking the hens. And I mind all the eggs being packed to be ready to sell, too. It's funny how it all comes back suddenly now I start talking about it. I loved the country."

Helen also remembered how her Granny used to cut her hair: "I had long blonde hair in those days, she'd cut it for me before I went back to school, it was always a really bad cut."

Helen and her brother David, by the 'market garden'

Hearing this story and looking at her now, it's extraordinary to think of the changes that have taken place in her life. Helen Lamb is part of the LBC1936 cohort, so is now 76 years old. Her short white hair is well-cut, she is smartly dressed, with long varnished nails and gold rings on fingers of both hands; she looks youthful and fit, and is living in a bright semi-detached house in the West of Edinburgh, near the Gyle.

This is the first time we've met, but there is no awkwardness when I arrive – I'm swept inside, and immediately caught up in a whirl of talk and laughter. On the fridge in the kitchen and on the walls of the sitting-room are photos of her good-looking grown-up children and grandchildren, and throughout her conversation it's clear that family and friends are the most important part of her life.

Helen's parents were the first tenants of the house in Carrick Knowe. "Mum was in hospital having me on the day Dad got the keys for the house. When they were first married they stayed in a tenement Meadowbank-way. I had friends who were all brought up in town in the tenements, and we used to get together at the weekends. I remember they were talking about going to the wash-house and I said, 'I've never been in a wash-house' - Mum had a big tub and wringer at home

- and they looked at me with their mouths open. 'Oh, you're *really* posh, then!' "

"We had a huge garden - it was a corner house - and it backed onto fields in those days. Dad loved gardening, it was like a wee market garden, a beautiful garden, all veg and flowers. Gardening was his life. There was a big red store-van used to come round - my Dad used to barter, 'I'll give you rhubarb to sell if you give me ....'. I had a very happy childhood staying there. Dad built like a wendy-house for us, with windows - and we'd play for hours with our dolls and prams."

Childhood summers: summers at the poultry-farm, summers at home: "I remember the summers – it was double summertime and the days went on for ever. They'd let us run wild – I can remember us giggling and hiding behind walls when it was time to go back in. We had this old pram, and we'd fill it with bottles of water, and bread and jam, and we used to trek up Corstorphine hill by the zoo, for the whole day. There'd be a crowd, sometimes ten of us. It used to be all fields right from here to Glasgow, just about! There was a farm, and a burn – and we used to walk with this pram for the whole day, playing, running wild."

Helen in her lace jabot

"I remember a lad fell off this tree, and we put him in the pram and wheeled him home. It turned out he'd broken his arm. We were only nine or ten years old at the time."

Helen left secondary school when she was fifteen, in 1951. "I couldn't get away from school quick enough. There weren't the sorts of jobs there are now and when they asked 'What do you want to be?' I didn't know, but I had a pal who went to be a telephonist, so I said 'Ooh, I'd like to be a telephonist.' Then I went for an interview for a job in a factory over in Leith but it was about an hour in the bus and I didn't like the dyes and the smell when I got there, and I thought, 'I'll no' wanna work here, it's not for me.' The Youth Employment people came to school and mentioned the 1951 census was going to need people to punch in the data, and I liked the sound of that."

Helen's parents encouraged her to go for an interview: "They said, 'If you get into the Civil Service, that's a really good job!'." And when, after the interview she was offered the job at a wage of £2 19s 6d a week, they were even more pleased. "My Mum said, 'Gosh, you're lucky – that's a lot of money'." She was given six weeks' training, working at a keyboard and punching coded information onto cards. "If it said 'male', that was a '1', so you punched in the '1'. We got really fast."

Then she was moved to Register House for the next two years. "What a laugh we used to have – a crowd of us would get in the train [from Corstorphine to Waverley]. I can remember running up the Waverley steps! I couldn't walk up them now!'

Her next job was at the 'Drop Centre' for the Civil Service, where she and others had to sort and file boxes of doctors' cards. "I think all the old dearies downstairs had mixed them up – they were always tutting at us. The man who was our boss nearly had a nervous breakdown, he was like someone from Dickens, really old, with long white hair." (He was probably all of sixty – if that!)

One day Helen and some of her colleagues took a half-day's leave to go to the ice-rink. "There were about ten of us hanging on to each other in a chain, and I let go and shot right across the ice. What a mess, grazes all up my leg and arm! But when I went back to work, the woman in charge looked at me and told me she'd been going to send me that afternoon for an interview for a government job. She said, 'Look at you! You can't go like that. Go home now and get tidied up'."

Helen got the job: it was in the 'Comp pool' at Government Building (now called Saughton House). "They trained me on a Comptometer Machine. It had a keyboard with numbers and we learnt how to add, subtract, multiply and divide – manually, not like now when you enter figures and just press a button for the answer! It was very interesting work, we used to do work for most of the departments in Scotland, like Health, Education and Agriculture – and part of our work was running a check on the figures compiled by the computer. Computers were huge things in those days, unbelievable. It was great work, I loved it. There were about fourteen of us in the Comp pool – again, they were very happy times, we had some good laughs. We worked *machines*, so the clerks looked down their noses at us. But they couldn't have done *our* work!"

(Helen has a great sense of humour, it comes bubbling out of her, and she is constantly laughing or clapping her hands; one leg, then both, are hooked over the arm of her chair by the end of our conversation.)

During her time in the 'Comp pool' she met and married Alan, and she left the job in 1961 "because I was pregnant. In those days you didn't go back when you had children. When I got married we stayed just two blocks up from my parents, and had the family [three sons and a daughter] there; then we moved here just on my fortieth birthday. I've been in this house thirty-six years!"

Helen went back to work in the Comp Room in 1975 when her youngest son was seven. "I had the four children but was starting full-time – my Mum stayed down the road, and she helped out, so it worked out fine. The beauty of the comp pool was that it was flexible – we all helped each other. Then my boss suggested I go for promotion, for a clerical job - and I got it. I wasn't sure if I wanted it because it was in Salaries, working with figures again. I went off on holiday and when I came back there was a letter asking me to go for another interview, doing coding! So it was like going back in time but on the other side of the fence – doing the coding not punching the cards. It was at the General Register Office, and we compiled the tables for Marriages, Births and Deaths for the Registrar General's Annual report. I was lucky because I was also doing the tables for the divorce rates and drugs-related deaths."

These words – 'lucky', 'interesting' – are recurrent themes in Helen's account: "I've been really lucky all my working life. I've always tried to look on the bright side," she says later.

When Helen started the job, "It was like being back at school. I was terrified of the old lady who was teaching me 'cause of death' coding, I felt like a fifteen-year-old! All of a sudden I was the new kid on the block, when I'd been used to being in

charge. I used to lie awake at night worrying."
But when she was finally due to retire, she was asked to stay on for another eighteen months, to help with the comparison between manual and computerised input.

Helen's husband Alan died twelve years ago, on 25th March, "on the night of my birthday. It was a Saturday night. Everybody had popped in at some time in the day, and everyone saw him and he was fine. In the evening we were having Chinese and he wouldn't eat Chinese. I asked what he wanted and he said, 'You know what I'd really like – haggis and potato and turnips'."

"I went away up round to the butcher's and I made what he wanted, and he was pleased – 'Oh that was lovely.' We were all sitting having our tea and my son shouted through from the kitchen, 'Dad, do you want some more cake?' And I was saying, 'Don't you eat it all now!', and when I looked across at him, his cup was tipped, like this," (she tips her empty coffee mug to show me), "and I asked what he was doing ... He was away. Just like that."

Alan had had two heart attacks previously, when he was only in his forties. "They took the feet from under him. He was a worrier as such, worried how I'd cope if anything happened to him. We all used to be careful around him and one day I said to him, 'We can't all tiptoe around. Is this how our life's gonnae be from now on? The bairns have been brilliant but this can't go on.' It did jolt him out of it and he lived another twenty years." He got a messenger job for the Civil Service: "He enjoyed what he was doing and his last three years were happy. But [his death] was horrendous at the time, coming with the shock as well as of losing him.' Then I thought, well, we've just got to get back to life as normal."

In the same way that Helen's mother looked after her grandchildren when Helen went back to work, Helen has helped with her son's children who stay close by.
"I'd look after the children on Tuesdays when my daughter-in-law went to work. I'd get up at 6am and go over - get them ready for nursery, then school. I thoroughly enjoyed it, I loved it - it was nice having them on their own and we had some good fun, they were never any trouble. My daughter said, 'No wonder, Mum, they'd be feart of you.' I didn't let them get away with much. But they're going to school on their own now, so I'm redundant!"

Helen Lamb at home 2012

"I'm quite lucky with the way my family have brought up their own families – that they realise things cost money. They've got more now than we did, of course. We all had an evening looking back at old photos and slides. I was a great knitter – all the boys had the same colour jumper, because you bought the wool in bulk, didn't you? They were all dressed the same, same colour trousers too. My son saw it and said, 'You never dressed us like that? That's really awful!' I said, 'For one thing, I could find you all – that's mine .. .and mine ... and mine!' I knitted them hats too and they saw the photos and said, 'Did you *really* think that looked nice?'."

Helen learnt a few medical terms about heart disease when she was working in the General Register Office: she rattles off ‘myocardial infarction’, ‘ischaemic heart disease’ as illustration. “We did learn quite a bit of medicine. Dr Susan Cole – the name’s just come back to me – was our medical adviser and she’d come to the office every week to sort out any queries we had regarding ‘cause of death’ coding and so on. Dr Cole asked if I’d like to come to Glasgow with her, and of course I said yes! We went through to the University, to the Forensic Department – we were sitting in this room, with rows and rows of bottles with odd-looking bits and pieces. But the meeting was great, I really enjoyed it.”

And how does she feel about finding herself now on ‘the other side’ in the Cohort studies? “The cohort thing is wonderful. You’ve got a full medical. And the IQ test – that was really funny. They asked me, ‘Do you want to know your results?’ and I thought, ‘Ach aye, why not?’ I actually did better! And last time I was there I got exactly the same mark. It’s very good, it’s very interesting.”

As for remembering the logical details in the ‘two stories test’, she laughs and stops playing with a rubber band to clap her hands: “I remembered more when I was going home in the bus than at the time. The second time I said to the girl, ‘Can you give me your mobile number and I’ll tell you the answers later’. I can remember names from forty years ago - then I can’t remember the pairs of words [in the test]! I’ve got four lines to learn, for a service that a friend’s organising. I’ll learn one at a time and maybe two hours later, see if I can remember them. And then I’ll be going ‘How does this start again?’.”

Helen was asked whether she would have her brain scanned by MRI, but she wasn’t sure because she’s “a bit claustrophobic. But then I thought, 'What an opportunity.' My son said, 'They'll have a hard job, Mum - is there a brain there?'!"

Helen in the Eastern Star Chapter Cabaret

The scan takes nearly an hour and a quarter, and it's cold and noisy inside the machine, but Helen found a way of coping.

"I belong to the Eastern Star Blackhall Chapter. Ten years ago I was top dog, the District Matron in Eastern District Grand Chapter. There's a lot of ritual, and I learnt it all. At the installations, I used to learn the pages and I'd stand there doing the installation, saying it word for word. I can still do it. It helps to keep the mind active." So when she was in the scanner, she thought, "Right, I'll start at the beginning, and I started going through the ritual in my head."

"Our Chapter is very homely, I made some very good friends. I went away to Benidorm with them every two years for a week in March. I had nights out and sleepovers – women in their fifties, having sleep-overs! We'd go to each other's houses, set the drinks out, go out for a curry or a chippy. That's what life's all about!"

"My partner John—" she gets up and shows me a photo; they make a very handsome couple, "—his sister was part of our Benidorm crew. He joined Blackhall Chapter. One of

my friends was having a Diamond Wedding and asked me to bring a partner...
I wondered whether to ask him, and I could see him going for his coat, so I went over and said 'How would you like to partner me?' He said, 'I've not got my diary, I'll have to have a look. But give me your phone number.' I thought, *'Oh!* If that's not a brush-off!'."
But Helen and John have now been together for eight years (he lives over towards Leith)."Friends say 'When are you getting married?' But we say we're quite happy as we are. He's a lovely man," Helen laughs. "I'm fighting the other women off!"

They were obviously meant for each other: both born in 1936, within eight days of each other, both members of the Eastern Star – and it turned out that they were both taking part in the Cohort study.
And, as Helen tells me, "I'll always end up speaking to anyone – and John's the same. I get on well with people. I like to feel I can help them."

"I can honestly say I've had a happy life. I loved my schooldays – I hated sports but I was happy and got on great with the teachers. I was Captain of the class – but I couldn't have cared less, I never had great aspirations to be top of the tree or anything like that."
As we wait for my taxi she tells me a funny story about trying out contact lenses instead of spectacles, ending with, "So I shoved the bottles across the desk at him and said, 'You can take your contact lenses, I'll no' be bothered with them'."
When the taxi comes we're still laughing ...

February 2012

Alison Pattie

Research Assistant, CCACE

Alison and the 'origami' hat "It came flat and you had to fold it to the right shape"

"I got into doing this by luck - I was a paediatric nurse before this." Until 1980, Alison Pattie looked after children who had cystic fibrosis or coeliac disease. That was "in the days when nurses looked like nurses - we had the apron, cuffs, black tights,and hair up under a stiff hat. A hat was totally impractical in the Sick Kids' - you'd put someone in the bath and they'd be reaching up and pulling it off your head!" She was a Staff Nurse, but now she laughs in amazement: "I look back and think, I was just a wee girl, and how did I do that?"

Alison left nursing when she became pregnant with the first of her three boys, but after thirteen years of looking after the family she wanted to go back to work. "But I wasn't sure what to do. I thought, 'I can't do nursing again, it's changed too much'." So, she moved from one demanding career to train in another: in 1994 she enrolled on the degree in Health Science at what was then Queen Margaret College, and graduated in 1998.

Sometimes the course of your life can change through unexpected interactions. She has been friends with Professor Ian Deary's wife for a long time: "I lived around the corner from her, and at that time we were both child-minders, and several of us would meet for coffee in each other's houses, with our buggies and the kids." Alison was invited to the Dearys' house for dinner. "We were chatting about what I could do and Ian suggested I apply for a job they just had coming up, a Research Fellow post. Martha [Pollard] got it, but as she was still working somewhere else part-time, Ian asked if I'd do a job-share with her. It was quite fortuitous. And then, in 1999, I became a Research Associate for LBC1921."

Alison was in from the start of the Cognitive Ageing project, and she admits, "At the beginning I found it a bit nerve-wracking because I'd no experience of research. I was a rookie! But at least in research you're not going to kill anybody!"

The 'Wave 1' testing of the 1921 Cohort was carried out at the Western General Hospital. "We did Wave 2 on a shoestring, at the Princess Alexandra Eye Pavilion because the staff there did the retinal photography. Alan [Gow] tested fifty people, I did nearly three hundred, in a wee horrible room, the grottiest room imaginable." But by the time the third Wave of testing came round, the team had moved to the new Wellcome Trust Clinical Research Facility at the Western General Hospital. "We can do the retinal photography ourselves now, it's amazing how quickly we mastered it [during the LBC1936 study]. When we apply for funding, we have to think of a new approach for each Wave. It was the retinal photography for Wave 2 of LBC1921, and for Waves 3 and 4 we've been looking at 'fluctuating asymmetry', the way the symmetry of the head changes. So I've been measuring ear height and width, and the wrists and fingers." She refers me to the work on fluctuating asymmetry from St Andrew's

University, and related work looking for correlations with health and intelligence or general mental ability.

Alison during the testing of the final Wave 3 LBC1921 participant

During the past twelve years, an enormous longitudinal data-set has been built up about the spread of medical histories, life-styles, genetics, and changes in cognitive ability of the people who are voluntarily participating in the Lothian Birth Cohort 1921 study. As Professor Deary says, "We're looking at a 'lifetime of intelligence'." These data are valuable and useful, not only to the groups actually involved with the project, but to other research groups internationally. "People are mostly interested in certain *types* of the data we collect," Alison explains. "Ian is quite meticulous about checking things, it all has to be double-checked – and as a result our data is quite clean. I double-check my own, and someone else does it afterwards too." Although she is occasionally self-deprecating, she is clearly deeply involved in and knowledgable about the project, and her empathy with the LBC1921 participants, whom she has known for years, is immediately obvious (and very much appreciated – see 'Margaret McKie's story', for example.)

Despite the importance of the LBC1921 study, many of the associated posts - including Alison's – are short-term contracts, yet she is remarkably relaxed as she talks about this."One year I was on three-month contracts! The final one had finished and they had a going-away party for me, with all the group (it was much smaller then), and they gave me a leaving present. That was on a Thursday. Then the very next day, the Friday, we got news of another grant and I was able to stay on." She laughs, "Ian said 'You'll never get another leaving do'!"

When the LBC1921 project first started, there were about 550 volunteers; now, for Wave 4, only those participants with perfect attendance have been invited back, about 160 of them and all now in their early nineties. Naturally, many of this age-group have impaired hearing or sight, which could potentially cause some difficulties. Alison explains that participants can use large-print texts if they prefer. "But a lot of mine are deaf – I'm bawling at the top of my voice." I comment on the thin walls of the rooms at WTCRF, and their proximity to the waiting area, and there's warmth and humour in her voice as she leans forward to tell me, "It's absolute murder if they're deaf! I try to test them on a Monday when there's nobody else around – but Linda [the receptionist] will say, 'I could hear you were shouting again the day'."
Alison is employed on the project for four days a week. There were three researchers working on Wave 3 but, "For Wave 4 I've just done everything myself – so if anything goes wrong, that's me! I do tests three days a week at the clinic or at a participant's home. There's lots to do. I like to be busy. There's lots of wee things as well as testing, like writing the invitations for appointments, writing to the GPs, sending the blood test results, phoning for taxis ..."

She is very aware that, of the 1921 Cohort participants, those who are doing well are the ones who have kept active, in brain and body, and who have friends and are sociable. She says she has taken note of this as regards the way she lives her own life.

Of her three boys, the two youngest (aged twenty-six and twenty-four, both in the legal profession) still live at home, and the girl-friend of one of them lives there too. "It's great - it's nice to have girlie things around, it's fine, quite a lot of fun. It would be a bit quiet without them."
"I don't drive, I like to walk everywhere - I can walk to work. On my day off, Fridays, I'm a creature of habit, I go to the gym - Anne [Deary] goes too and leaves her grand-daughter in the crêche, and then we all have breakfast together afterwards."

As for her job, Alison says she really enjoys the testing. "I've seen the same people several times now and I know them quite well. Some of them are so nice. One woman brings me a black pudding every time! They send us Christmas cards, and we have this competition between the LBC36 and the LBC21 teams to see who gets the most. We've got far fewer participants, but we have about ten times more cards." She laughs again. "They have their wee pathetic string...!"

February 2012

Thomas 'Tam' Young

LBC1936

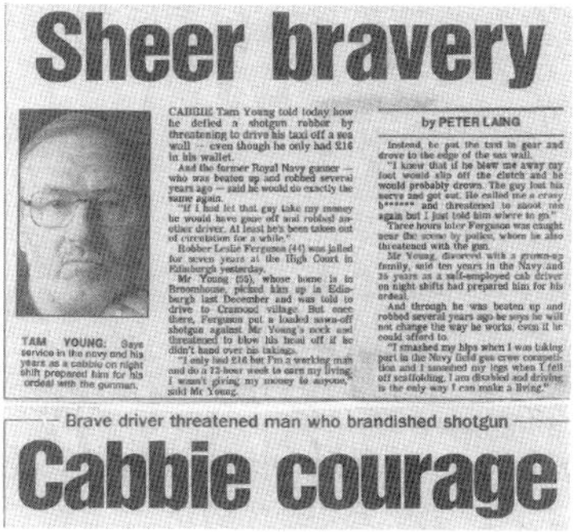

Sheer bravery

by PETER LAING

CABBIE Tam Young told today how he defied a shotgun robber by threatening to drive his taxi off a sea wall — even though he only had £16 in his wallet.

And the former Royal Navy gunner — who was beaten up and robbed several years ago — said he would do exactly the same again.

"If I had let that guy take my money he would have gone off and robbed another driver. At least he's been taken out of circulation for a while."

Robber Leslie Ferguson (44) was jailed for seven years at the High Court in Edinburgh yesterday.

Mr Young (55), whose home is in Broomhouse, picked him up in Edinburgh last December and was told to drive to Cramond village. But once there, Ferguson put a loaded sawn-off shotgun against Mr Young's neck and threatened to blow his head off if he didn't hand over his takings.

"I only had £16 but I'm a working man and do a 72-hour week to earn my living. I wasn't giving my money to anyone," said Mr Young.

Instead, he put the taxi in gear and drove to the edge of the sea wall.

"I knew that if he blew me away my foot would slip off the clutch and he would probably drown. The guy lost his nerve and got out. He called me a crazy b****** and threatened to shoot me again but I just told him where to go."

Three hours later Ferguson was caught near the scene by police, whom he also threatened with the gun.

Mr Young, divorced with a grown-up family, said ten years in the Navy and 26 years as a self-employed cab driver on night shifts had prepared him for his ordeal.

And through he was beaten up and robbed several years ago he says he will not change the way he works, even if he could afford to.

"I smashed my hips when I was taking part in the Navy field gun crew competition and I smashed my legs when I fell off scaffolding. I am disabled and driving is the only way I can make a living."

TAM YOUNG: Says service in the navy and his years as a cabbie on night shift prepared him for his ordeal with the gunman.

— Brave driver threatened man who brandished shotgun —

Cabbie courage

Newspaper article, November 1991

In 1958, Able Seaman Young was hit on the hip by the 120-pound wheel of a field-gun. He was part of a Royal Navy crew taking part in the field-gun race, a favourite event in the annual Royal Tournament at Earl's Court . The gun carriages are assembled and dis-assembled several times throughout the race, and when one of the wheels was being carried across on the steel wire, it collided with Thomas. "But I carried on. Every time I done a run, ken, my leg was collapsing." The navy's physiotherapist worked on it later, "quite forcibly", telling Thomas that "field-gunners don't feel pain"; but his efforts made things worse. Thomas was "moaning with pain in the night, and all the guys were throwing boots and shouting 'Shut up! We cannae sleep!'."

In the morning it was decided that he should go to the hospital to have his leg and back checked out, but he wasn't given any transport. "It was just, 'Able Seaman Young, where's your bike?'." So, he cycled the three miles to the Royal Navy Barracks, and after an X-ray was sent straight off to orthopaedics because his left femur was badly fractured. "They couldn't believe that I'd cycled there. They'd been saying, 'tell your driver to go away'."

He wasn't a good patient, even though his leg was in traction.

He had "a bit of a run-in" with the Ward Sister because she'd refused to let him watch a programme on television, even though his team was on; there was an altercation, with some physical violence and restraint, and the Surgeon-Commander was called and said, "You've gone too far. I'm going to have you sent to D-block with all the bampots" – or words to that effect. "I spent a day in D Block – that quietened me down," Thomas says, his eyes twinkling behind his glasses.

We're in his sitting-room at Forrester Park Gardens. I've had some trouble getting access to the flat because the front door to the close is locked and there aren't any bells. Finally a passerby rather witheringly tells me to go round the back, and I push open the garden gate, pass the bins, and gain access to the hall. The door to Thomas's flat shines with varnished wood, and I hear the clanking of keys and chains as he opens it. He explains that they have to keep the front door locked because the kids from the school opposite used the close to gather and eat their lunch.

The sitting-room is furnished with large dark-red leather chairs and a sofa, and on the shelf beneath the handsome wooden table there are boxes of games, box sets of DVDs, and Bill Clinton's and Barack Obama's autobiographies. Behind the door are shelves tightly-packed with books such as *'Did you know?'*, *'How is it done?'*, and encyclopaedias, dictionaries, the *Chronicle of Britain.*
Thomas points out the photos on the wall, of his first wife and of May, his 'common-law wife' as he calls her, and their children. There are photos of his own daughter, April, too.

There is also a framed document, a Meritorious Award, presented to him by the Lothian and Borders Police and

relating to his bravery on November 7th 1991. At that time he owned a black taxi, and late one evening he had picked up a man who produced a sawn-off shot-gun, held it to Thomas's neck and demanded his watch and money. Thomas kept cool and drove the taxi onto the quay at Cramond and, keeping his foot on the clutch and the engine revving, told the man that if he shot him, they would both end up in the water.
"He started shouting at me, 'Let me out, you mad bastard!' When you turn the tables, they're not that brave!"
The police caught the man, and the story hit the papers.

Thomas gets up and fetches a thick album of photos. He extracts a yellow envelope with a New Zealand stamp. It's addressed merely to *'Tam Young, taxi cab driver, Edinburgh'*, with a scribbled note asking the post to try to find him. Inside is a card from someone who owns a taxi firm, congratulating him on his bravery. He had read the story in his Scottish wife's newspaper – and the minimally-addressed envelope had reached Tam, half-way round the world!

Able-Seaman Thomas Young (back row, right) and other Grenville Division trainees at HMS Ganges, 1952

Thomas left school at fifteen, and in 1952 left Niddrie, where he had been born, to join the Navy as a 'boy seaman', training at the notoriously tough RNTE Shotley – known more usually as HMS *Ganges* – at Ipswich, in Suffolk. Why did he choose the Navy? "There was nae work, the only thing where I was, was in the pits, ken. Quite a few people I knew had accidents. I saw the Navy as getting a bit of travelling, getting around – in other words, freebies!" He remembers the big floods in that area in 1953, and recalls attempts at rescue work at Harwich. "We'd gone round in a cutter, and whenever we saw a group of seagulls, there was a body."

Trips at sea took him to places like Hong-Kong, Singapore, India and South America, and he briefly volunteered with the Gurkha Rifles in Malaysia in 1959, before joining the newly-commissioned warship HMS *Leopard* in 1959. "She was the only ship at the time with stabilisers. I used to suffer from sea-sickness, so the only reason I chose her was because of that."

That same year, Nigeria was granted independence, and *Leopard* made a courtesy call. On June 24th 1959 she navigated upriver to Port Harcourt. The British oil-workers and their families and friends welcomed her crew with a party and a free bar; there was much rejoicing and carousing and, when the drink ran out, the Scotsman Thomas Young with an Irish friend (their Welsh friend sensibly dropped out) decided they would walk to Lagos, where the ship would return in several days' time.

Earlier, shortly after I had arrived at Thomas's house, he had given me several pages torn out of a ring-bound note-book, on which he had carefully written the story of that decision and their extraordinary walk. It makes gripping reading, and I have included it at the end.

Thomas came out of the Navy after ten years, in May 1962. "I was still an Able-Seaman. I was the kind of guy that used to get into trouble." His eyes glimmer, with his quick smile.

He then worked for the Scotland Electricity Board "for a wee while. But then I discovered I'd make twice the money, ken, if I went into scaffolding. If we had to stay away on a job, we'd get paid extra, so I'd take my van, and I'd sleep in the van and keep the money. If we were out in the countryside we'd shoot and eat rabbits to feed ourselves."

But not long after, on December 17th, 1963, "I had a head-on collision with a ten-ton crane." The firm he was working for were supplying all the scaffolding for the new BP refinery, the petrochemical works at Grangemouth, and when he was driving his van back to town at night a crane reversed out of a field in front of him, without lights or banksman; Thomas did an emergency stop but hit black ice, and the metal box that held the dashboard instruments was forced back against his pelvic region. "I had compound fractures in my legs, lost my left patella, had a fractured pelvis and a fractured rib-cage." He was taken to Falkirk Royal Infirmary and was in a critical condition for three weeks, in and out of consciousness. "But we used to do a lot of jiving when we was young, and there was one time when I came to [in the hospital] and I heard music, Bill Bailey playing 'Shotgun Boogie' – and it brought me out of it, and that's when I started making positive moves to get better."

Determination – or perhaps sheer bloody-mindedness – is one of Thomas's characteristics. His left leg wouldn't bend and he wasn't supposed to put any weight on it, but he was determined to recover his mobility. "I got one of my friends to bring in a sand-bag, and at night when everyone was sleeping, I'd put my leg over the side of the bed and rest the sand-bag on the ankle." Of course the knee-joint swelled up like a balloon after doing that a few times, and when the surgeon discovered what he'd been doing, "He said 'If you're that determined to get mobility in that joint, I'll take you to theatre at the Princess Mary Rose [orthopaedic hospital] and forcibly bend it!' "

When he left hospital, he couldn't go back to scaffolding because he couldn't climb – but he *could* walk and drive, so he bought an old van and drove around selling fruit in the streets, soon making enough money to buy a bigger van, a mobile shop. Loading it with fruit and vegetables – including a half-dozen hundredweight sacks of potatoes, fresh from the small-holdings – he drove around the Schemes. "I used to sell that whole bin of tatties in a day. There'd be queues waiting. I brought them cheap food – I had a good clientele."
But eventually, it was the carrying of heavy bags that caused his right leg to collapse inwards below the knee. He tells me how he drove to the hospital out-patients, and the consultant who saw him sent him straight off for surgery, for cutting and pinning of the bone. "So I realised I'd have to give up the van."

By then he was married; his wife had two children from a previous marriage, and they soon had a daughter, April, of their own. Thomas bought a black cab. Life was easier as a taxi-driver, but "to make enough money for a family I had to work night-shifts. That would bring in £20 extra, ken." For various reasons the marriage didn't work and, coming back early one morning, he found his wife "had done a runner with the girls". She got custody of the children and for a long time he only saw April three or four times a year.

Some time afterwards, he met May, and he has obviously told the story several times, because he is practised, amusing

– and still amused. May was a passenger in his taxi: a victim of domestic violence, she asked him to find her a bed-and-breakfast where she could safely stay. But the American aircraft carrier, the USS *Nimitz* was moored in the Firth of Forth, and "everywhere was full of sailors and prostitutes from Glasgow" (Where else? The Two Cities' mutual antagonism runs deep!). May tried her sister, then her brother, with no luck; "she was talking of throwing a brick through a window so she'd get taken into a cell for the night." "Eventually I says, 'I know it sounds funny, but I've got a spare room you can have for the night.' She looked at me and says, 'Do you think I came down the Clyde on a banana-boat?' But in the end she saw I didn't mean her any harm, and she stayed." He came off shift in the morning expecting that she would have left, but "the light was still on and she'd fixed an English breakfast for me." So May stayed on: she cooked for them both and paid "a tenner a week" in rent.

The ground-floor house, in Harrison, had had three spare bedrooms since Thomas's wife had left. "One day May said, 'Why don't we double up and rent the two rooms?' " Thomas laughs as he tells me this, and sits up straight. "She had a great business head on her. She was the best thing that ever happened – you could trust her."

Later Thomas sold the Harrison house and they moved to Forrester Park Gardens. His relationship with May and her own children was often complicated, but they were still living together when she died, more than four years ago.

When April was older, she started to visit him. "She said, she'd heard all these things about me for so long, but now she needed to find out for herself." He has constantly

supported her: he paid for her to get lessons in Greek and Italian. Fluent in Greek, she moved to Greece and taught English for seventeen years; he bought her a flat with some of the money from the sale of his house. More recently Thomas supported April through a two-year MA in Applied Linguistics at Portsmouth University. (The proof copy of her thesis arrived a couple of days before my visit, and he fetches it for me to look at.) She wanted to find a job in England, he says, but gave up and has now gone to Sicily to work.
"All the investment I've made in my daughter, it's paid off – she's *established*."

Thomas looks steadily at me as he talks; his face is serious but when he smiles his whole expression changes; occasionally he gestures or rubs his knee. As his conversation becomes more intense, he remains standing, speaking directly at me. There is an anger simmering beneath the surface, an anger at injustices done to himself and to others, even people in far-away places that he has visited, like South America and Africa.

"I used to write a lot," he says, "especially to the government – Thatcher, Heseltine, and other politicians ... I wrote to Michael Heseltine in 1992 about the closure of twenty-one pits. In 1985 I wrote to MP Hurd about the destruction of the Scottish industrial base, in Ravenscraig and the strip-mills. This was the era of Maggie [Thatcher] stripping Scotland's assets and compromising our ability to compete in the markets." He fetches a bundle of letters, to show me, all of them replies. "I got long pages back, about foreign policy and the like."

Not only writing a lot, but reading, too: in the taxi, doing sixteen-hour shifts and a seven-day week for five years, he had plenty of time for reading, mainly the *Reader's Digest* because he could read it in short bursts. And for a while after he retired in 2001 he was a member of a Book Club.

I ask him about the DVDs on fishing and it turns out this is a fairly new hobby. "I go fly-fishing with the man who bought my taxi – I've been doing it about three years. When I started off, ken, the only fishing I'd ever done was sea-fishing in the Navy, off ships!"

Tam Young at home

Despite his "two game legs", as he calls them, he says firmly, "I've never claimed disability."
He points to the exercise bike in one corner of the sitting-room: "I used the bike until recently for an hour a day. I like to keep my muscles flexing – and hard breathing is good for the heart muscles. That and the garden is my only exercise – I do the front and back, and the guy next door's too."
And he tries to do a "Five-minute memory work-out" – he waves the small booklet – every morning to keep his brain healthy. (He even has a 'system' of numbers for the lottery.)

With regard to the Cohort study, Thomas says, "I feel that I'm doing something useful, ken. I'm making a contribution to the common good." He's already decided to donate his brain tissue.
"And the surgeon who looked at my leg not long ago said he'd never seen anything like it – all the cutting and pinning!

He said, 'I'd love to get that leg – could you send your left leg to the orthopaedic unit at St John's?'!"

"You can only die once, thank God!" Thomas is smiling widely. "And everybody's talking about recycling ..."

October 2012

State visit to Nigeria 1959
An account by Thomas Young

It was hot and humid with a mist being burned off by the tropical sun as Her Majesty's warship HMS Leopard *berthed alongside the oil terminal at a still-sleeping Port Harcourt.*
It was 6am on a Thursday in June 1959 and the frigate had arrived on a courtesy visit, where the 'Brit' workers living in an isolated compound eagerly anticipated the visit as the social highlight of the year. Onboard the seamen secured the ship and lowered the gangway in readiness for the first liberty excursion ashore.
At 1600 hours the single-decker dropped the grippo crewmen at the oil compound in an isolated forest area, where we were advised by the workers that all alcoholic beverages were free, which was gratefully accepted by thirsty crew members.
It was a night of social cohesion, singing, dancing, including a 'conga' by all members through the compound and the swimming-pool, as we endeavoured to drink the compound dry. Alas, after four hours and a severely depleted bar stock the bar was closed, and fond farewells and new friendships were made as we prepared to return to the ship, with a slight list to port!
Meanwhile Able-Seaman 'Brigham Young', a Scot, and Able Seaman 'Delaney Coyne' *, an Irishman, discussed the possibility of a Scot and an Irishman exploring the Niger valley on foot. Approximately 300*

miles through swamp and primary jungle, from Port Harcourt to Lagos, a formidable journey at this time of year, the dry season, when predators come into contact with villagers.

In a moment of passionate pride and bravado the intoxicated pair made a momentous decision to trek on foot from Port Harcourt to Lagos where the ship would be berthed.

The two stalwarts left Port Harcourt before the transport arrived, and made haste with a quick-marching routine to distance ourselves from the compound. After marching for four hours in pitch blackness we came across a small kraal of six huts and decided to ask for shelter.

On our entering the compound, the inhabitants began to shriek and wail in pure terror, and we couldn't communicate, and feeling exhausted we lay on the hard ground in the village and fell fast asleep.

We were woken the next morning by chanting and singing, and prodded vigorously by a large lady with a stick. We surfaced in the bright sunshine with formidable hangovers and an insatiable thirst, which we successfully conveyed to the large lady. The headman of the village was honoured to have such distinguished visitors from QUEEN Elizabeth's Navy and offered unlimited hospitality.

That afternoon the Headman introduced us to everyone individually in the village and was at pains to explain the rejection the previous night. The huts are barricaded against predators and ju-ju people, and two figures in tropical whites who suddenly appear from the blackness was terrifying to superstitious people, but he was missionary-educated and above superstition.

It was late afternoon and we gratefully rejected his further hospitality and said our goodbyes to the villagers, and with a full stomach we took to the road cheered on by villagers and ridiculed by seniors, who fell about laughing uncontrollably.

By late evening we passed through Aba, where we purchased two loaves of white bread and two large bottles of lemonade and continued our journey followed by young cyclists for 3-4 miles, who were highly amused. We forced a speed march for 30 minutes and a normal march for 30 minutes, to cover distance before nightfall.

The night came down suddenly and swallowed us up in an inky blackness and a feeling of isolation and apprehension and, realising the absurdity of our foolish predicament and the dangerous environment and strange noises, we decided to arm ourselves with stout sticks. We found a high perch in an accessible tree, which was safer than sleeping on the ground, but within the hour we were attacked by large red ants and abandoned the idea, deciding to go through the night thus avoiding the severe heat of the day as our only source of liquid was almost depleted. We marched abreast in the darkness, singing sea-shanties to bolster our courage and hopefully scare predators!

At last a break in the cloud formation and the moon lit up our immediate vicinity in a silvery-grey tone, visibility improved and with it our confidence. We speeded up our march on the red dirt road, avoiding clumps of tangled undergrowth spilling out into the narrow road. Suddenly I caught a glimpse of something ahead of us, moving in stealth mode, and alerted 'Delaney' who armed himself. We stopped and headed for a large tree to possibly avoid a predator but a bright snatch of moonlight identified the movement of three Africans carrying pangas and who, having lost the element of surprise approached us warily demanding food, drink and any valuables in broken English in a threatening manner.

With our backs to the tree we swung our clubs to keep them at bay, but a vertical lunge from the ground narrowly missed the underside of my left jaw, and both of us realised instantly that this was a life-or-death situation. We counter-attacked with a burst of energy that surprised them but they re-grouped and tried to get behind one of us, things looked bad for us. In the distance was the sound of a revving heavy vehicle, the three bandits stopped for a moment and launched a concerted attack just as the headlights of a Ma-Ma wagon came into view at speed.

The three bandits were silhouetted in the headlights and the truck screamed to a shuddering halt, the driver jumped out and fired a double-barrelled shotgun over the heads of the three who vanished into the undergrowth. The driver, wearing an ex-army shirt and sporting a medal ribbon, had served in the British Army in the Africa campaign. He literally saved our lives and gave us a lift into the nearest town, Oweri. Oweri was our watering-hole, and fed, washed and watered with a few hours' sleep, feeling refreshed and more confident, we decided to carry on and hopefully accept any lifts in the direction of Lagos.

We left Oweri early evening with water and sweets to supplement energy and, aware that onboard Leopard *we were A.W.O.L., if we gave up we would go back losers, so we decided to go back winners.*

We made good time and dropped the speed-marching which burned up energy and stamina. The road was better-surfaced and level and boosted morale being closer to bigger towns.

Well after 1am in pitch darkness we heard the noise and movement of numerous large animals and had serious doubts of surviving the night. We heard a car engine approaching slowly, it came into view, an old Ford model with spoked wheels stopped, and out stepped an African Church of Scotland Minister.

He'd awakened at midnight with a strange dream, he was told 'tonight you are called upon to be a good Samaritan', he knew two people were in mortal danger and it was imperative that he act at once, which he did. 'Delaney' and I sent him a Xmas card with the ship's crest.

PS The Minister dropped us off at another oil compound but the Brits in the compound, believing we were deserters and shaming the flag, called the police, who arrested us and drove us back to Lagos to join the ship and face disciplinary action.

(The story was written about 14 months after de-mob.)

[*] Nicknames: "In the Navy, your surname determines your nickname and you don't have a choice in the matter. So 'Young' becomes 'Brigham'. 'Dez' acquired his because of his drumming skills, after the big-band drummer Delaney."

Dr Mark Bastin

Reader in Brain Imaging
Department of Clinical Neurosciences
Western General Hospital

"I have a twenty-minute walk to get here – it's wonderful to walk to work and when you go home the walk helps to clears your mind. Or to see problems in a different way."
Today, hot and sunny, is a good day for walking anywhere: when I arrive Mark, wearing casual trousers and a white short-sleeved T-shirt, has been sitting outside in the sun, at the top of a small concrete path behind the department. He has already put out a second chair for me - which I soon have to move into the shade of a tree. "I'm English," he grins, "Whenever the sun's out I like to be in it." We laugh at the sudden and unseasonal display of bare legs and chests in the parks and streets (the following week it snows). Buds are opening on the trees, and across the road a blackbird is singing. The large air-conditioning plant next to us occasionally roars into action.

Mark in Edinburgh 2012

As well as walking to work, Mark goes running and occasionally cycling: "The trouble with working in the medical sphere is that you get to see so many diseases! So I know I need to work at keeping fit". He tells me about studies comparing how physical and mental exercise affect the brain structure, which found that the continued integrity of the brain may be more dependent on physical than mental activity. He cups his hands and moves them in a circle so that I can almost see the imaginary brain – "Imagine the millions of blood vessels in the brain – physical activity helps perfusion to the different regions. It's obvious that good physical exercise as well as good diet is important."

A quick read of Mark's university webpage shows an impressively wide-ranging academic background: "*Dr. Bastin graduated from the Universities of York, Edinburgh and Oxford with degrees in Theoretical Physics (BSc Hons), Remote Sensing (MSc) and Geophysical Fluid Dynamics (DPhil). He then pursued a long-held interest in medical imaging and magnetic resonance techniques by joining the Magnetic Resonance Spectroscopy (MRS) Unit in the Department of Biochemisty, University of Oxford, where he worked on skin and cardiac MRS methods for 4 years.*" Then, fifteen years ago, Mark moved to Edinburgh to a post as Research Associate to work on magnetic resonance imaging (MRI) of the brain; within a year, in 1998, he was made a Lecturer, and in 2006, he was promoted to the post of Reader in Brain Imaging.

Now, with the MRI work, he explains that he's interested in "playing with the MRI scanner and getting it to do what we want." The scanner here in the department has a magnet with a strength of 1.5 Tesla. "Modern machines have greater strength. Our scanner dates from the late 1990s, so we have a physical limitation on what we can see because of the magnet's strength."

One of the main aspects he works on is "writing computer code to process the data, so we can generate biomarkers for brain integrity. This means we want to look at the relative volumes, how the different areas are connected, the integrity of the white matter and the connections to the cortical regions."

Is he then a computer geek? He laughs, leaning back in his chair and relaxing in the warmth of the sun.
"I've *always* been interested in computers since I was less than twelve – even then I wanted to be a computer programmer. It's nice to get a computer to do what you want - and to get it to generate different images from numbers."

Looking at his degrees and research interests, I think that it's not too difficult to see how he has pulled together these various expertises to home in on imaging analysis and MRI. But the topic of his doctoral research in 'Fluid Dynamics' turns out to be a surprise. "I was always interested in astronomy and the universe, especially when I was younger," Mark says, and he gained his PhD for modelling the theoretical processes that create atmospheric patterns and flows of gases around the large planets. "If you think about the factors that affect flow, you've got spin – Coriolis' force – and you've got differential heating, from the core of the planet or on the surface with heat coming from the Sun. So we had a large spinning rig, where we could heat the centre, like in Jupiter or Saturn, or we could heat the walls, to mimic solar heat." Again using his hands to sketch out the shape, he explains that there were boundaries at the top and bottom of the rig that simulated curvature of a planet. The fluid around the rig contained minute polystyrene beads, illuminated at different levels to pick up the differences in flow, and the whole structure was surmounted by a rotating camera.
He goes off to his office and quickly returns with his bound thesis, flipping through the pages to show me the diagrams of flow patterns: the different cells of rotation under different flow conditions are dramatic – one of them where the fluid is rotating within a stationary cell, like the Great Red Spot on Jupiter. He is enthusiastic, a good explainer, easy to talk

and listen to, and – as with all successful research scientists – clearly open to new ideas, and generous with praise where he feels it is due.

Of the multi-disciplinary Lothian Birth Cohort study he says, "They're a good bunch to work with. There's a range of different competencies, all feeding off one another – you've got psychologists, radiologists, radiographers, physicists, computing scientists ... It's been interesting having to learn each other's languages. I firmly believe that knowledge is always good, and worth striving for, whatever it is. You never know what spin-offs will come out of it, what serendipitous findings."

The study generates such a huge amount of data – how is it possible to analyse and make sense of it all? "It's so well-characterised, there's so much information coming out. That's what is so nice about working with the psychologists, they combine the different data-sets and they test their hypotheses with statistical techniques – such as how different factors are inter-related, and how they affect each other. If you phrase the question correctly, it's possible then to pick out the data that can help to answer it." And in addition to the group meetings, "about three times a year we have wider meetings, where the entire 'community', if we can call it that, meets to discuss the progress."

The LBC project is important, not only as an overall study on cognitive ageing, but also for MRI research, in that it is providing a longitudinal study of different individuals in the ageing process. " We're now re-scanning some of the participants. The radiographers have noticed that after the second Wave there's been a decline, there's more deterioration, they're more fragile and less able." By comparing the scan results with the cognitive tests, "Can we point to important factors that relate to how well a person ages cognitively?"

The imaging is a long process: a couple of the LBC1936 participants have talked about the length of time, nearly 75 minutes, that they have to remain in the scanner. "That's both good and bad. We generate lots of data, but we might also be putting people off. " Naturally, the participants talk to each other – Eddie Dishon, for example, told me he had the full-length scan but that the man before him had had a much shorter session. Mark says that if there are real difficulties, the radiographers can cut down on the different types of imaging. "We just use subsets rather than the whole programme – we'd prefer to have something rather than nothing! And in the end, we want to gather as much information that is as useful as possible for as long as possible. New techniques are always being developed, and in the future might allow re-analysis."
Of more general importance too, in terms of studying the brain, is the fact that the techniques they are developing for the LBC studies can also be used across different patient groups, such as those with Motor Neurone Disease, stroke and Multiple Sclerosis.

Mark enjoys supervising the PhD students in his research group. "They're adults, they know what they want to do, and what they want out of it. I get lots of feedback from them and that's valuable – they're the engines of all the research, and they're always coming up with new techniques." As a Reader, he has more time for research, which is clearly what he most enjoys, for as he says, he is "more of a practical person, I like to get my hands on things."

One problem about research in Edinburgh, not only in terms of funding but also getting the right people, is that "recruitment can be difficult. The cutting-edge stuff is done in the Golden Triangle [London, Oxford, Cambridge] and people's perceptions are that Edinburgh is just too far out of it."
But despite this, he says, "I love living in Scotland and I love the Scottish people. You can chat to people in shops and it's not considered a sign of weirdness as it is in the South [of England]. I worry about going back to live in England, I'm not sure I'd want to."

His wife – whom he met in Oxford – speaks French fluently, and they and their two daughters often tour around the North and middle of France. Mark says they talk about living there eventually, "We plan to rent a place and to see how that goes for a while. But there's a dilemma in that I realise that as we get older we'll need more support. When I'm sixty-five my perpectives might be different about where I want to live!"
The little villages they so much like in France are very similar to those near Oxford. He occasionally cycled round the Oxfordshire countryside when he was working on his PhD, and he and his wife also liked to drive to the Cotswolds. "We had a little green Metro, and we chugged around the Cotswold villages, round all the Slaughters, the Chippings – Norton and Campden ... I love it, the Cotswolds are one of my favourite places. The villages retain a mediaeval charm that's been lost elsewhere in England."
Does he walk or cycle in the Scottish countryside? No, he says, he finds the Scottish Highlands are "too lonely and alien". But then, he *was* born in Watford!

Every so often, as just recently with Ian Deary and colleagues' paper on genetics and intelligence, the cognitive ageing work hits the national media. "I even had my own fourteen seconds a few years ago on Channel 4 News when they came and did a piece on us!" Not fifteen? He laughs. "Fourteen-point-seven then, on Channel Four News in October 2008!"

We discuss the way in which science and scientists are depicted in the media and on science programmes on TV. Mark is firmly of the opinion that it is always good to have science talked about because "money is so scarce and science is often undervalued." We talk about the continuing efforts to improve public 'appreciation' rather than 'understanding' of science, and Mark says, "I feel very strongly that we've got to get the message across. Science is a force for good – it benefits the whole of mankind."

March 2012

Margaret McKie

LBC1921

It's mid-February and crocuses are opening their blue and yellow flowers in front gardens along the street. In Mrs McKie's back-garden, bullfinches, chaffinches, blue- and great-tits and a fat, waddling wood-pigeon are busy around the seed-feeders hanging from a tree. The tubs on the small paved area outside the sitting-room patio doors are still damp and wintry, but Mrs McKie has already been looking through her Thompson & Morgan plant catalogue, planning which flowers she will order. She smiles as she tells me that she now buys plant-plugs instead of seeds, because the rewards are so much faster. "I can bring them on the back room if I need to – it gets very warm in there whenever the sun's out."
From the patio there are steps up to the lawn and greenhouse, beyond which is an area that has been cultivated for vegetables. Although Mrs McKie doesn't grow tomatoes or much in the way of vegetables any more, she was a keen gardener when her husband was alive; there are shrubs and trees, and the back garden catches the sun most of the day. It's good to imagine it ablaze with T&M's flowers in the summer: the waist-high wall by the steps is an ideal height for planting up the tubs and pots.

She has lived in this house – a neat semi-detached bungalow with a dormer window in the roof – for sixty years: two-thirds of her life. It's hard to believe that, as a member of the 1921 Lothian Birth Cohort, she is 91 years old. A tall, upright and smiling woman, she had welcomed me warmly, leading the way - with a slight limp - into an attractive sitting-room that was furnished with a dark-green leather suite.

After her husband retired, they had occasionally discussed whether they would move house, but they always concluded that they would stay put. "It just suited us so well and we had no reason to move. I love the countryside, but whether I'd like to live there, I'm not sure!"
She'd had experience of staying in the countryside, because her husband's parents ran a small-holding in Ayrshire; the family would holiday there when the two girls were young. "But we never went abroad with the children. After they'd left, my husband and I usually had one holiday abroad each year, usually a coach tour somewhere." She went to Ireland for her grandson's wedding: "But that was the last time. I don't go away at all now, and I'm not going to – I'm quite happy being here."

Mrs McKie at home

Mrs McKie was born in the Abbeyhill area of Edinburgh, then her family moved to the Merchiston area so that her parents could look after her grandfather. From secondary school she went to work at the Department of Health. It was while working in the Civil Service that she met her husband-to-be. "He was from the country. And he had been working in London from 1939 to 1941. That was not a good time to be there! The move to London must have been traumatic for him, he was only seventeen years old. Then he came back to to Edinburgh and he was in the Civil Service too, which is how we met."

In common with most women of that time, Mrs McKie gave up her job after her marriage, and much of her domestic life revolved around that of her girls and her husband. " When the children were young they went to Craiglockart School, where I used to go as well. It's only about four minutes on the train. They came home for lunch – my husband came home too. All the children from this area were allowed out fifteen minutes earlier, at twelve, so they could get the train home for lunch. If I wasn't in the living room when they came in they'd be calling 'Mum, where are you?' Of course it did mean that I always had to be here at lunchtime."

She studied for her Highers at Boroughmuir Secondary School, but chose the 'Lower' maths option because she always found geometry difficult. "But I could cope with maths. I like algebra and to this day I use algebra to solve problems. I went up to Wick to see my family, and my grandson was struggling with his homework. I said I'd help and he gave me such a pitying look. I did the problem for him and said, 'I get such and such' - and it was right." She beams at me. "I said to him, 'I'm not as stupid as you think!' "

'Gardens of Scotland' cross -stitch picture

I express surprise that she wasn't keen on geometry, because there are three hand-stitched tapestry cushions on the sofa, and several framed cross-stitch pictures on the wall, one of which is a very modern representation of tulips and lilies; she clearly has a 'feel' for shapes and spaces. She has always enjoyed sewing, but explains, "I don't do so much sewing now, partly because my eye-sight's not so good at ninety-one. I've had to tell people not to give me any more – I was running out of space!"

Talk of geometry and shapes leads naturally into talk about some of the tests for the Cohort project, and Mrs McKie laughs. "Yes! The Moray House test! I can remember doing the original one [when I was eleven]. They told us at the time we wouldn't know the results, but now I know – and I've done it three times since. I get between ninety-five and one hundred percent, my score hasn't changed. But it's the sort of thing I love doing – I love puzzles and things like that. I still do the '*Scotsman'* crossword – and this!" She pulls a small wheeled drawer-set towards her chair, and brings out a large Puzzle Compendium. She laughs again when I accuse her of practising for the Moray House test. She has really enjoyed her involvement with the Cohort study, she says, and especially the interaction with the researchers such as Alison. "And what we appreciate very much is that we each get a newsletter at Christmas and a card. They have all signed the card, and it makes a big difference, we so appreciate it."

Playing sport been important for most of her life. "Hockey, badminton, tennis - and then I was bowling until seven or eight years ago. When I was expecting our first daughter, my father said 'that bairn's going to be born with a badminton racquet in its hand'."

To play bowls you need to be able to bend your knees, and the reason for her limp is now explained. "I had to have a new knee about two years ago and I asked the surgeon for his honest opinion whether it would help at my age. He said 'You're going to go on until you're hundred', so I should have the operation. I said to him that the problem with the knee was probably the result of playing so much sport so I had no regrets. But I'm not competitive, I don't enjoy having to be stressed up all the time. I played strictly for fun, it was very relaxing."

Did she have to wear whites and a hat for outdoor bowls? "The greys and whites, the skirts, even the hats? Oh no. Thank you - but oh no! We just wore whatever suited us. Sometimes it was so cold at the start of the season and I had so many clothes on I could hardly bend!"
Exercising started at an early age, but was not always welcome. "When I was growing up my father had a sedentary job so he felt he had to get some exercise of an evening after he came home. He made me and my brother go out for a walk every evening after tea. We hated it - after all, we hadn't been sitting around, we'd been busy in the day. Even in the winter, we had to go out, in the dark. We used to ask ourselves, ' What was the *point*?' "

On Sundays the children were definitely not allowed to wear 'whatever suited'. "We had to go out walking as a family after lunch. In the morning there was church, then we had Sunday school, so it was a while before we even had lunch. My brother and I would walk in front, and we used to long for a wet Sunday so we could stay in. We had on our Sunday clothes, and I had to wear a hat. It was a black velour hat, with a band that had the school colours (we didn't have a strict uniform in either of the schools). Then in summer the band went on a panama hat instead. We'd go walking round the streets and meet other families. We were not allowed to do anything on a Sunday except *read* - no knitting, no sewing, no piano. Sundays were not enjoyable. I can remember feeling terribly guilty the first time I went to church without a hat - and that was when I was grown-up! To a certain extent I'm still hidebound in that I don't ever wear trousers to church - that's the one day in a week I don't wear trousers, I wear a skirt."

The local church has played its part in other ways. It was through a friend from primary school days who also attends that church that Mrs McKie found out about and volunteered for the Cohort study; and for a couple of years she played the piano for the church's musical group when they were putting on shows. "I play well enough to enjoy it, and I can read [music] pretty well. Another friend lives in sheltered housing and she organised a little choir, ten or twelve people keen on singing, and I'd play the piano for them. They'd get together once a fortnight and put together a little performance for the inmates twice a year." Humour glimmers continuously as she talks, but she has a delightful strain of pragmatism too. "We did our swansong last Christmas - it's the nature of the place, people were dropping off and they were down to about four. So we had to call it a day!"

I stand in the kitchen doorway while she makes tea, pouring it into pretty pink-flowered china cups. There is a *'Nota bene'* tea-towel hanging on the side of a cupboard, which a friend had bought for her ("*Piano,*the neighbours have complained; *Obbligato,* being forced to practice; *Crotchet,* knitting; *Rubato,* ointment for the musician's back" ...). She puts out biscuits and buttered home-made drop-scones on more of the matching china. "I still like baking. I always did my baking on Friday, and I remember one of the girls coming home and saying she was envious of a friend because 'she gets shop fancies all the time!'."

Despite her knee, Mrs McKie is very active, and makes me laugh when she says, "I like to be independent, though I get into trouble sometimes from my family, especially if I do things that mean going up a ladder." But living where she does has caused one or two problems: "Transport's difficult from here and the hill is becoming difficult – I can't cope with a long slow haul, so I need quite a bit of help in that respect as I can only carry a small amount. Milk is a particular problem because it's so heavy. I used to have my milk delivered but it kept getting stolen, especially on a Saturday, so I had to cancel it."

Her husband died twelve years ago, but although her grandchildren are dispersed (she also has four great-grandchildren, with another due this summer), her daughters still live in Edinburgh, and often visit and do her heavier shopping. "I'm very lucky to have them so close – the younger one still phones me every night at six o'clock. I know the phone will ring, and I keep telling her she doesn't need to, but she always says, 'It's just so I know you're all right'."

Next to me is a framed photo of a tiny sleeping baby, a seven-week-old great-grandchild, wrapped snugly in a woollen cardigan and shawl. "We got full marks from the midwife for that! She told my grand-daughter that they always liked handknit at the hospital. I still knit – but only on demand because not everyone wants hand-knitted clothes these days. But I do a lot for the wee ones, wee jackets, bootees, hats. I knitted the shawl, and that was very demanding - three times I made a mistake and had to rip it right back. But it was a joy when it was done."

Later, Alison Pattie, the Research Associate who is

responsible for the 1921 Cohort, tells me that when volunteers from both the 1921and 1936 Cohorts are at the Clinic, she sometimes finds it hard to guess which age-group each belongs to, because so many of those in their nineties are still so lively and fit. Mrs McKie certainly falls into that category.

Just before I leave, she says something that makes us both laugh: "The church also has a Friendship Club where people over fifty can get together, and it's packed out every week. I get invited once a year to play the piano for them. They keep inviting me to join, but my daughter says, 'Oh Mum, you're not ready for that yet.' It's not my scene, quite honestly I *don't* feel ready for it, though I do have the greatest admiration for those who run it . And then I think, oh *no!*" – she claps her hands over her face and laughs – "You're an arrogant so-and-so!"

February 2012

Mary Agnes Brown ('Maisie')
LBC1936

"'I'm pretty ordinary, I worked in a shop, window-dressing." I have barely found my pen and notepad before Maisie Brown ("Nobody calls me Mary") sits down opposite me and launches into her story.
Her husband Jim stays in the room although, as he explains to me, he is very deaf; nevertheless he watches and listens, and at one stage brings out a very relevant file of photos. Maisie is energetic, leaning forward to emphasise a point, leaping up to bring things to show me, animated and smiling.

She was a window-dresser for ten years, then left when she had their daughter, Linda, she explains. Five years later she went back to work, to Melrose's in Princes Street. "Then they closed down." Then she went to Swears and Wells, where she was a sales assistant and window-dresser, selling mink coats and other furs. "Then they closed down." Next was a leather shop ("And they closed down") and finally to Singer sewing machines, where she worked initially in the fabric department before moving on to selling the machines. "I was on commission so I made quite a lot of extra money. But then Singer's closed down and I got my ten-year service badge and my redundancy notice in the same week!" By now we're both laughing. "Oh! And the church Jim and I were married in closed down too!"

Maisie's life started at Abbeyhill, but then her family moved to Leith when she was very young. Unfortunately Leith, because of the docks, was targeted by German bombs during the War; and there was also the incident of the landmine. "I was slightly injured when the landmine fell on Leith. We lived in a tenement, and for some reason the shelter was locked, so when the siren went off we went down to the bottom flat. Then the landmine fell, and the concussion blew the fire out into the room. I had my gas-mask over my shoulder and a furry animal hanging from it, and I threw my arm up to protect my face. Afterwards we found the animal was burnt – I was lucky, it had saved my face – though I had to go into hospital overnight."

As a joiner, Maisie's father was in a reserved occupation, but he was in the Docks' fire-service and out on call when the landmine fell. "My father came home and he didn't know where we'd all gone, he was really worried. The place was a terrible mess, the windows were out. It wasn't completely wrecked but everything had been blown about by the concussion, part of the ceiling had fallen into my brother's cot."

The family went to live with an aunt in Marionville, just South of Leith, and Maisie remembers that when they went back to look at their house, "father put on the radio, and the first thing that came on was the song, 'You'd be far better off in a home'!"

From Fort Street Primary school, where she sat the Moray House test ("I vaguely remember it – and being fairly good at it") she went on to the Leith Academy. But she left school when she was sixteen.

"My mother had mental health problems, so I was kept off school a lot to look after my sister. I knew I wasn't going to get Highers so I left. I was always good at art, and somebody said that would be useful in window-dressing, so I thought, well, I'll do that."

She now fetches a folder of pencil drawings, and sorts

through them, holding them out for me to see. They are portraits, mostly copied from photos – Sean Connery, 'The Man from UNCLE' Ilya Kuryakin, Kirk Douglas – and are very good likenesses, cleanly-executed. There is also a drawing done from life, of a much younger Jim, without a beard and wearing glasses. Maisie stacks the drawings on her knee. "I haven't picked up a pencil for a long time. I'm trying to get back to it but there's so much else to do, now I'm looking after Jim."

Jim has had an artificial heart valve since he was fifty-two years old, and two years ago he developed macular degeneration (when I leave he tells me that he can see the stripes on my tunic – and Maisie, who is also wearing a striped jumper, says she now always tries to wear bright colours on his behalf). Concomitant with this loss of vision, he has visual hallucinations, a condition known as Charles Bonnet syndrome. And as if this were not enough, Maisie adds, he also had a gall-stone operation a year-and-a-half ago which "went wrong", leading to four more hospital visits. "But we're coping, aren't we?" She leans across to him and repeats it, and he agrees.
She is officially a carer, and has joined the Carers' Support Group, *Vocal*, which helps carers find out about NHS equipment and other entitlements; for example, Jim has an alarm on a wristband which he wears when Maisie has to go out. And their daughter Linda and her husband, who live in Drumbrae, a couple of miles to the West, are now retired, so Linda comes over "to help out" with the house-work.

Jim and Maisie have been married for fifty-four years. They met when they were both working at Leith Provident, and moved to a rented house on Albert Street in Leith. "We knew

everybody on the stair," Maisie says. But the building was bought by a landlord who "filled it with students" and, of course, the ambience changed.
Linda had heard about Roseburn Place, and suggested they might consider moving to one of the retirement flats, "So we came to have a look, with our cheque books, and we decided on it there and then!"

Portrait of Maisie Brown as a young women

We have been talking about Linda, and Jim opens a folder of photos. I go over to his chair to look at them: there is a photo he took of a younger Maisie, looking stunning, peering back over her shoulder in a film-star pose, and one of Linda. I say that she is lovely, and Jim says quietly, "I think so too."
Maisie fetches a framed photo of their grand-daughters, and my comment that they look almost Spanish with their dark hair and high cheekbones, makes her laugh. "Well, that's interesting you should say that. Jim's from Westray in Orkney and you'll probably know that one of the Spanish Armada ships was wrecked there. Some of the crew survived and married islanders, and their descendants – they're clearly different in appearance, they're smaller and darker – are known locally as 'the Dons'. Jim's mother –" she fetches another photo from the china-cabinet – "looked very Spanish, she was small and dark, and people used to say to Jim, 'Oh, you're one of the Dons'."

Maisie and Jim have lived at Roseburn Place for eleven years and it's not at all surprising that they made such a quick decision to move there: the attractive block of McCarthy & Stone flats, with a warden and communal facilities, has a garden and benches and bright plants in pots at the front, and is next to the Water of Leith and the playing-fields around Murrayfield Stadium.

There are plenty of communal activities too, Maisie says. There are concerts (Linda's barbershop quartet amongst them), film and quiz nights, and there's a monthly afternoon tea. "I'm sociable, so I go to most of the things that happen – I leave Jim in peace": she smiles at him again, and he nods.

Although Jim retired when he was sixty-five, Maisie worked until she was seventy. "I was part-time only, and only worked on Saturdays at the end. I always was part-time, even from the start. I've got a lot of hobbies, and I never wanted to work full-time otherwise there'd be a lot less time to spend on them."

Earlier I had commented on several turned objects on the mantelpiece, all small and delicate and in a dark, but light-weight, foreign wood. "My dad did wood-turning, and so did his brother. We're just a family that liked making things." She herself has always "made things". She used to make toys (there is a rabbit, and teddies and other toys around the flat), and glove-puppets, and dressing-up clothes for her grand-daughters.

From early on, she was enthusiastic about teaching other people to make things, too. "When I was at Singer, I had to teach people how to use the machines. That's what I most liked doing. I got really friendly with some of the customers, and I took over a wee sewing class, a lunch club on Thursdays at Westerhailes. I just liked showing people how to use the machines."

She set up a patchwork class at Roseburn Place, "but some of them gave up, and I had to finish most of the pieces myself! At Christmas you can still see some of the wreaths they made on their doors."

"I decided I'm not going to go on doing that if I have to finish the things myself. So then I set up a knitting class, from 7.30 to about 8.45pm on Fridays. We put away £1 every week and when we had enough we all went out for a meal." But there are only five of the original twelve members left now – "it's the nature of the place, that numbers decline" – so she has recently put up a notice in the hall to let newcomers know about the class.

Maisie and her 'Grandmother's Fan' patchwork quilt, 2010

Maisie used to belong to two quilting groups, and still keeps in touch and tries to get to their exhibitions. She takes me into the bedroom to look at one of her patchwork quilts, and some smaller versions of the five full-size bed-quilts that she has made: the green, cream and purple 'Carolina Lily' pattern, the intricate array and rich russet-based colours of 'Log Cabin'. "I've got to use up the material, I had such a lot. One thing I've learnt, if it's going wrong, use the scissors and put it in the bucket!"

She uses a small table in the sitting-room for her sewing, she explains, and as we go back into the sitting-room, she becomes more serious. "I've been under a lot of strain with looking after Jim – I've had to learn take over the finances, as well, which has been a bit daunting – and the patchwork shuts me off. It releases me." Making quilts might have other uses too: later, when she is talking about the pattern-recognition tests in the Cohort study, she says "I'm probably good at it because of my patchwork. That's what has kept me going through this horrible couple of years."

Although she admits that she doesn't go as often as she used to because she doesn't like to leave Jim for too long, she still has some light relief with the Leith Choir. "I'm an alto, and though I used to sing solos I don't enjoy that very much any more, so I do recitals instead. The recitations are funny, Scottish ones mainly." My puzzlement is obvious, so she explains further: "We put on events, where the programme is three songs, a solo, three songs, a recitation, three songs, a solo. We all get turns, I recite maybe twice a month."

This has extended recently to reciting *Tam O'Shanter* at the Roseburn Place Burns' Nights, and she laughs as she says, "It's quite exhausting, but I'm a big show-off, I enjoy doing it!" It's a long poem, needing a good memory. "Oh, I've a good memory for that – but I can never remember where my keys are! But I *can* remember conversations and especially *where* I've had them. I have a very visual memory. When I'm reciting a poem I know what part of a page I'm on."

She heard about the Cohort study from a friend, and says she has thoroughly enjoyed being involved. "I've done the written test twice. The results for the one I did at school were in the 'respectable' range, and then I got similar and higher scores in the last two. I've improved! I like doing puzzles and things like that, such as crosswords and Sudokus – I try and keep my mind going." She finds the test sessions long and requiring a lot of concentration but, with characteristic humour, she says, "I said, 'You're testing us to destruction!' " And, having had two brain-scans, she has recently decided to donate her brain (*see note at end*).

Maisie and Jim Brown in St Andrew's

Although the dark-green leather swivel-chair in which I'm sitting is comfortably enfolding, Maisie says that they are having to get rid of them and that two new armchairs are due to arrive in a couple of weeks' time. She laughs, to belie her words, when she says, "I cried most of one day at the idea of not being able to get out of these chairs!" And it's hard to believe her when she says she's finding it difficult to get up and down stairs – "that's when I feel my age" – because she is so active during my visit, both physically and mentally. Her determined optimism is uplifting.

"Looking after somebody you love is not quite the strain of looking after someone else – that would be awful. We get on pretty well –" she checks with Jim, reaching across to touch his knee, and he nods again. 'We yell at each other sometimes, don't we?", she laughs again, "But I've never been hungry, I've never been cold, I've always had people around that loved me. We're no' wealthy or terribly successful, but we've had a good life."

October 2012

Note: With regard to brain donation (see above) Professor Ian Deary explains: *"We have gained ethical approval for a Lothian Birth Cohort 1936 Brain Tissue Bank (LBC1936-BTB). For those LBC1936 members who are interested in taking part in this, as soon as possible after their death their relatives will call the 24-hour LBC1936-BTB number and a post-mortem examination will be arranged. Small samples of different important parts of the brain will be carefully taken and stored, and the rest replaced. There will be no obvious signs on the body of this having happened. The tissue will be valuable in years to come, we think, in telling us about the brain foundations of healthy cognitive ageing. We are fortunate that Edinburgh is the centre of the UK's Brain Banking experience and we shall benefit a lot from that."*

Donald Lyall

PhD student, LBC Research Team

The day before we met, Donald Lyall heard that a paper he had submitted for publication had been accepted by the journal *Behavior Genetics*. He is still excited about this, and rightly so: the paper is based on the work he carried out for the second chapter of his PhD thesis. Donald, part of the CCACE research group and in the third and final year of working towards his doctorate, has not one but three research supervisors, Ian Deary, David Porteous and Joanna Wardlaw, because his research "integrates the three modalities" of genetics, brain imaging and cognitive behaviour. All the data come from the ongoing tests on the Lothian Birth Cohort participants.

Donald Lyall

He is looking at the variability in two genes, known as *APOE* and *TOMM40*; *APOE* has what is known as pleiotropic effects – its product influences one biological process (lipid metabolism) which in turn influences other later processes – and has been shown to affect the development of the protein tangles called amyloid plaques in the brain, indicators of Alzheimer's disease. The product of the *TOMM40* gene helps certain proteins to get across the membranes of mitochondria within each cell. Donald looks at me anxiously, "Do you know about mitochondria? They're like the power-house of a cell."

Both genes are polymorphic, different people have different variants. "You can't say they're genes 'for' Alzheimer's, they're not, directly," he explains, " but there are two 'risk' variants, which indicate a risk of developing Alzheimer's."

Not only is Donald looking at variants of the two marker genes, but he's able to use the MRI scans of brains to analyse the connectivity of the tracts of white matter, the changes in size of the hippocampus (one of the first regions of the brain to suffer damage in Alzheimer's disease) and lesions in the white matter. "And then I'm finally putting it all together"—the genetic variability and the brain variability—"to see how these factors affect cognitive ability," he explains. I ask if this might not be seen as one of those exercises in correlations, like "men who carry umbrellas have heart-attacks" and he laughs, "You're right!" but, quite unfazed, explains that because of the wide reach of data collected in the LBC studies, it's possible to control for many other factors, such as the history of various diseases including diabetes and stroke. "We can look to see to what extent the gene variant is tagging along with some other disease, or another gene variant. We have good biological plausibility." He too is very plausible, adept at countering questions. "We're not just casting the net out and finding correlations, you know – I always make myself think, in testing a hypothesis, 'If *I* had to go and collect this data, would I be happy with it?' "

We are sitting in a corner of the Psychology Department's mezzanine area, the pale November sun streaming in and making intricate patterns of the ornamental balustrade. Donald – who was reportedly nervous about this 'interview' – now seems entirely relaxed, smiling often, leaning back in his chair, legs crossed, an ankle hooked over a knee. Occasionally he waves and calls "Hi!" to a passing acquaintance; his arms are constantly moving, gesturing, hands sometimes clasped over a knee; or interlocked in front of him, arms crooked, elbows out. Words come pouring out in his enthusiasm, but he occasionally stops to check if I've understood the science and whether he should explain.

Throughout our meeting, he several times repeats how lucky he is to be part of the LBC research effort. "I'm ridiculously lucky to have several hundred brain-scans. To have a data set like this is absolutely mental! There was a previous study using about a hundred and fifty – we have six hundred to seven hundred. Someone asked 'Is your study larger than all previous studies on this particular topic, combined?' and I said 'I think it might be'."

This, of course, is an important point: the larger the data set, the greater the probability that the conclusions are right, the more the hypothesis can be trusted.

"It's become a hobby – I'm always checking my emails to see if any new data's come in," and he says again, "I'm so lucky! My parents are always saying, 'If you enjoy this stuff and it's not work to you, why consider doing anything else?' "

Donald Lyall helping at the CCACE exhibition

When we start talking about his life in general, I'm soon smiling to myself. Who is interviewing whom? Donald's questions keep coming: What did I work on? How do I feel about the LBC project? What do I write? Which is my favourite of my novels, what is it about? Where do I live? Where did I live in Glasgow? When I answer the latter question he says he's envious, he loved his time in Glasgow. He was born in Glasgow, but his family moved out of the city to Fintry ("in the middle of nowhere"), then to Kippen ("even more the middle of nowhere") and from there to Callander in the Trossachs. "It was a great place to live, but not so good for a boy of fourteen, it seemed like the back of beyond." He went to school at the Dollar Academy near Kinross.

He wasn't at all interested in science, he says, and admits that he didn't work hard: "I was a lazy, stupid boy!" He decided that he'd apply to read Media Studies at the University of Stirling, but this was a subject for which it was notoriously difficult to be offered a place. A friend told him that it was easier to apply for "a random course, and when I get there, to ask if I can change", so he applied to read Psychology. "After I was accepted I asked if I could change to Media Studies and they said 'Nah'." So he read Psychology and English – "It was good."

After graduation, Donald moved to the Psychology Department in Edinburgh and did a Master's in Cognitive Neuroscience. Subsequently he wanted to move into clinical psychology, but prior to that, for about three months, he worked in a shoe-shop: "It was the *best* job, nine to five and I had to keep everything in order. It was brilliant, really good fun."

Then serious work took over, when he started to work with the Gorbals Addiction Service in Glasgow, helping people with anxiety and depression, and doing cognitive testing for alcohol-related brain damage (where the brain shrinks due to the effects of alcohol and malnutrition). "I loved my job," he says, "I loved Glasgow, and I really enjoyed my flat-mates."

But by 2010, he was keeping his eyes open for other jobs in psychology, and he saw the PhD opportunity at CCACE advertised. "I saw this post had brain-scans for seven hundred people available. *Sorry*? And I thought, I'll give it a pop!" He leans forward, elbows out, hands linked, to make his point. He says he "liked the idea of using a scientific approach about affecting the quality of life and the health of people. It has an order to it—" (like tidying a shoe-shop?) "—and it has humanity. I like the fact that it's both detailed and also uses a bit of intuition."

When he came for interview for the post, he and Ian Deary (his supervisor and Professor of Differential Psychology – *see also Ian's story*) apparently spent some time talking about bands. "We also talked about headphones – I didn't realise at first how much of a music nut he was!" Ian subsequently sent him a list of "about a hundred" bands he should listen to. The common interest in bands arose because Donald, as an undergraduate at Stirling, set up a music society with some friends. "It was another of life's stupid twists of fate," he grins. He had two friends who were musicians but didn't often get to play gigs, so they decided to set up a society. They found a promoter and approached the Students' Union. "We had a deal where we offered three bands for three quid, every two weeks. The bands got a crate of beer and the chance to show off. We made hundreds of pounds. It was just cool, doing stuff. Just fun."

But this meant that Donald had to spend time going around

to listen to bands. "One thing it taught me was that within about thirty seconds you can sense whether the band is any good. I probably learnt something from that, for introducing myself at conferences – in just thirty seconds you need to get your ideas across."

Now, outside of work, he goes running most days, "for fun", and he's recently taken up hill-walking. "I wasn't prepared for just how ...." he searches for the word "...not exactly *demanding* it is, but hard. I have my own Theory of Relativity. A cup of tea halfway up a hill is—" he makes an expression of delight "—but a cup of tea in the office is, well, just a cup of tea."

Back at CCACE he doesn't work only on his own research project, but is also doing the administration for the current round of brain-scans on the LBC1936 participants. "I do some of the cognitive testing, I help out, so I know the data is very carefully collected. All this data at my finger-tips, it's such a ridiculous opportunity! But it didn't just fall out of a tree. So I needed to understand what goes into it [in terms of collection and analysis]. That's why there are lots of names on the paper*, it's not just me and my supervisors, but also the people that get the brain-imaging data, the genetics people ..."
.

"I read about doing a PhD, that you get out of it what you put in. I spend a lot of time on seminars, posters, digging-in – and it's exponential what you get out of it. But you're also part of a community – you have a laugh with people."

November 2012

ADRB2, brain white matter integrity and cognitive ageing in the Lothian Birth Cohort 1936, *Behavior Genetics*, *in press.* Donald M. Lyall, Lorna M. Lopez, Mark E. Bastin, Susana Muñoz Maniega, Lars Penke, Maria del C. Valdés Hernández, Natalie A. Royle, John M. Starr, David J. Porteous, Joanna M. Wardlaw & Ian J. Deary.

Eddie Dishon

LBC1936

"I tend to have an excessive hoarding attitude but I think that it is due to how I was brought up as a child, where I was brought up and the nature of my employment. I was born in a lighthouse (1936) and as there was no local shop round the corner, my father taught me not to throw things away in case some day they would be useful. This can obviously get out of hand, but as I grew up, people would come and ask me if I had this and that to help them out as they knew that I might still have one!! I am now retired, but finished my working life as an engineer with Northern Lighthouse Board automating the lighthouses in Scotland. As I am sure you will understand, there are no DIY stores handy to lighthouses and so my hoarding was quite well known around the Lighthouse Service. Again, if a part required repairing, it would often be "Ask Eddie, he might have something suitable tucked away somewhere." This has reached the stage of me not being able to get the car in the garage, and there is hardly a tidy room in the house, but I still think that if a disaster happens in the house, I can at least make an effort." Eddie Dishon, Scotland, commenting on *'Why some people become hoarders'*, BBC News Channel, December 2004

Eddie Dishon and I are having a cup of coffee in the bright waiting area of the Wellcome Trust Clinical Research Facility at the Western General. He has a broad and engaging smile, especially when he talks about his hoarding. "I can't even get into my garage – Channel Five got hold of me for a programme they were doing, but I refused. They wanted to see what was in the mind of a hoarder."

Eddie and his mother sunbathing at Mull of Kintyre lighthouse, 1936

Eddie ("I've never been called Mister, I'm too silly for that!") was born in 1936, in the lighthouse on the Mull of Kintyre, where his father was a Lighthouse Keeper. When his father moved to different lighthouses around the Scottish coast, Eddie and his mother and brother moved too. Of course, the family didn't live actually inside the lighthouse – there are cottages for the Keepers' families, with walled gardens and outhouses, and Eddie tells me, "To this day I still remember the smell of marigolds and lilies – someone once said to me, 'well, think how tall you were then – the flowers would be right at your nose'."

He is tanned and looks fit and relaxed and at ease with himself, casually but neatly dressed in a shirt with small blue, white and brown checks, grey-and-blue striped socks, and dark trousers. Although we have not met before, he is instantly engaging, very open, with "nothing to hide" (as he says himself); ready to joke,especially with the nurse, and pleased to talk about his life.

At 11.45am, Catherine Murray, one of the Cognitive Ageing project's Research Assistants, takes us to the small room that is used for the tests. Eddie is very concerned for my well-being, re-arranging the chairs so that I have the one with

arms, asking if I want water. Catherine starts with questions about his health (I check again whether they are happy for me to stay), and when asked about his level of activity, he says, "Basically I just run around." "Have you ever been told you have dementia?" she asks, and he replies "I forget." He looks round at me with a mischievous grin, and I try to keep a straight face when he is told to ignore me.
Questions follow about diet – salt alcohol intake and so on - and there are tests for hearing and memory; there is a series of commands that test his understanding and dexterity; and tasks on the computer – onscreen simple shapes which are then hidden, so that he must decide whether the longer line was on the left or right, and respond by pressing the corresponding button. Towards the end, the test becomes increasingly difficult as the pictures are hidden ever more rapidly: looking over his shoulder, I find I'm struggling too.

I take a break and when I go back in, forty minutes after Eddie has started the session, Catherine is checking the life-style questionnaire that he has completed at home. Eddie says that for so many of the questions he picked a neutral response, "Because I kept thinking, 'it depends ...'."

(This reminds me of an observation that Dr Martha Pollard, the Senior Research Associate previously involved in three 'waves' of the LBC21 testing, made: "I've noticed that more participants question the questionnaire than previously. Their answers aren't clear-cut. Often they're saying *'it depends...'* There's an interesting tension here between what is truly important in someone's life and what is expressed in data.")

As to his equivocal answer to the question about whether he considers himself soft-hearted, Eddie explains, "People wonder why I pick up a spider and put it on a piece of toilet paper to put it out – and I say, 'well, I might come back as a spider'."

At about one o'clock, we stop for a lunch of sandwiches, apple juice and tea, provided by the Centre; Eddie is again very insistent on looking after me, that the first choice of the sandwiches should be mine.

During our lunch-break, he tells me about an experience he had when he was in his forties, out on the Dubh Artach Lighthouse "There's nothing there but the rock and a heli-pad, and we couldn't get off at the end of our shift because of the weather, allegedly the helicopter couldn't land because the sea was breaking right over the helipad. They asked the RAF for help, but they wouldn't come out either, so we ended up staying there for four-and-a-half days. We were working inside at the top when a message came through saying we'd got just half-an-hour before a helicopter came out from Prestwick to get us. We had to clear up, get our survival suits on and wait on the balcony."
By then he had himself been working on lighthouses for several years, and was well-used to being transported to and from work by helicopter, but this time it was not so simple. "One of the crew came down on the rope and told us what to do. There's a tail on the rope and you mustn't touch it because of static, it has to be earthed first. If you touched it before that you'd be *away*! The helicopter was hovering above the top of the lighthouse, and there was a big risk of its rotors hitting the tower – and I was thinking, 'If I'm on the rope and that happens, then – *ping*'! "

But eventually all the team were lifted up into the air and taken to the depot at Oban. Afterwards, and much to Eddie's disgust, "The Daily Mail made a big story of it, and it got reported everywhere. We hadn't wanted to come off – we had food, we had work to do and we just wanted to get on with it."

He still retains a few memories of the first years of his life at the Mull of Kintyre lighthouse. During the War his aunt and girl cousin were evacuated from the city to join them; at Christmas, a shoe-box would arrive containing presents, "always from the same lady". One time he was given a big pedal-car. The lighthouse was on a steep hill, with a 200-foot cliff beneath, so it was fortunate that the keepers' houses were enclosed by a wall. "I can remember driving the car around in the living-room, and the mudguard ripping the imitation-leather armchair – that was the end of the pedal car in the house." One night during the War when he was being put to bed, there was a commotion outside and voices, saying something was on fire. "I stood on a box up at the window and could see a ship floating, on fire. But I don't think I knew what happened after that."

On the day the family moved to Orkney, deep snow covered the ground. The car that came for us couldn't get down the hill and we had to carry everything up to it. I didn't want to leave and I have a memory of being dragged through the snow, roaring my head off – in a howling gale. His father had been appointed as a Keeper out on Sule Skerry, forty miles to the West of Orkney Mainland, to which the Keepers had to be transferred by the service boat. Eddie and his mother stayed on dry land, in one of the Keepers' Cottages in Stromness, where Eddie started school. "I can remember a few

things. There was a camp at the back of where we lived, filled with soldiers. And I can remember seeing the fleet in Scapa Flow - and there was a Prisoner-of-War camp" (probably for the Italian prisoners, who painted the *trompe l'oeil* murals in their chapel, the converted Nissan hut by the Barrier).
It was here in Stromness that his mother nearly lost him. He was feverish with a sore stomach: "The local doctor said 'Rub his tummy and give him castor oil', but for some reason my mother knew that could be fatal. We took a taxi all the way to the Balfour Hospital at Kirkwall" – in those days it was a collection of converted Nissan huts – "and a Polish surgeon with a wooden leg told mother he didn't know whether he could save me." His mother wasn't allowed to visit him, he could only wave to her through the window, but the nurses "stitched a chamois cloth on my teddy Rupert, and filled it with cotton wool, so he had his operation too." Hygiene was a different matter in those days: "One time, a nurse said,"'Make yourself useful' and she gave me a pile of cotton-wool and asked me to make swabs for the theatre! Can you imagine?"

Eddie and Rupert the teddy, after their hospital stay

Approximately five years later, the family moved again, to the lighthouse on the Butt of Lewis. Eddie's wife Norma tells me later that his mother had told her that "the Principal Keeper's wife ruled the roost." Eddie remembers that "when the van came, the Principal's wife was always out first. She might stock up on all the chocolate biscuits and tea, then the other wives had to take whatever was left." He shakes his head at the memory: "Sometimes the hatred was atrocious."

That year, surprisingly for the Outer Isles, there was snow, and Eddie decided to make some skis. He knew where he could acquire a couple of curved barrel staves and some six-inch nails; he told his younger brother Brian where to place his feet then hammered the nails into the wood around them. "I tied his feet on with string and hauled him to the top of the hill – though when I went back later the hill didn't look nearly as steep – then pushed him off." (Later, Norma says that Brian often used to complain, "Why does it always have to be me that tries out Eddie's inventions?")

The stay on Lewis only lasted a year, because his mother had to spend some time in hospital in Edinburgh. Eddie and Brian stayed with an aunt in the city and he was enrolled at Granton school, which is where he sat both his 11-plus exam and the Moray House intelligence test. By then his father had been moved to Noss Head lighthouse at Wick, where the family soon joined him.This was one of Eddie's favourite homes: "I remember helping on the farm just up the road by finding the wayward lambs at lambing time, and at harvest time being proud as Punch at being allowed to drive the new Field Marshall tractor up and down the field while the "grown ups" forked the sheaves up onto the trailer. Eleven years old, and driving the best tractor on the farm!" But after three or four years, Eddie's father was made Principal Lighthouse Keeper on Duncansby Head at John O' Groats, so the family moved again – this time, Eddie's mother moved back down to Edinburgh with the boys so that Eddie could finish his schooling, at Trinity Academy. He completed about three-quarters of the academic year at the local school, then, because he would be fifteen in August, left school at the end of the summer, aged fourteen.

That September, 1951, Eddie began work at the estate agents, DM Hall & Sons in Edinburgh. "It's a big firm now but there were only about six of us in the company then – and I was the office boy." He had the possibility of learning how to carry out house-surveys, but he "wasn't keen" and left after a year. "I wanted into engineering, and I started my apprenticeship in about 1952 with Ferranti's in Edinburgh. I did five years there, then in 1957 I was called up for National Service. I was an instrument technician in the RAF and ended up working on Shackletons in Northern Ireland until 1959."

Eddie removing the last section of the original navigation optic lens assembly, Ailsa Craig

In 1972, aged thirty-six and after spending nearly thirteen years "wandering round the world", Eddie joined the Northern Lighthouse Board as an engineer. Initially on the maintenance team, he later shifted to helping with the automation of the lighthouses around the Scottish coast and on the Isle of Man. "The others would say to me: 'You were born in one, and now you're getting rid of them!' We'd take everything apart. We stripped out the prisms, then we'd rig up a crane and bring the pieces down. We had to have everything tied in a cargo net ready to hook on when the helicopter came."

He worked for the NLB for thirty years, often heading out in a helicopter from Stromness with his tools, and being "dumped in the middle of nowhere. I thoroughly enjoyed it. I'm not a city person. Take me and drop me in the middle of nowhere and I could manage, I'd be happy."

But this made family life awkward: most of the work in bringing up the children devolved on his wife Norma, especially during the months between Spring and Autumn. "When I was working in maintenance you went away for a month, then came home for a weekend, that was all. In the winter months, it was more of a nine-to-five job, because we had a workshop in the centre of Edinburgh where you would manufacture any of the bits and pieces that could wait until the following Spring. I remember I came back in the plane one time, and Norma and the kids came to meet me. David, the youngest, hid behind her, he didn't know who I was."

Our lunch-break now comes to an end, because the Senior Research Nurse, Joanna Munro, has joined us to take Eddie's blood and measure various physical parameters. Jo is cheery and relaxed, very ready to chat and banter with Eddie, which he clearly enjoys. Again, he insists that I stay and watch as he goes through the various measurements: height, weight, lung capacity. He reads the letters on the eye-test card in a strong voice and when told to walk as fast as possible down the corridor, walks very fast. Back in the small clinic room he has to answer questions about his activity at home - whether he goes shopping, can get onto a bus, the length of his reach, and so on. There is a breath test, and a grip test after which Jo congratulates him, saying "We had a young lad in his twenties who was a rugby player in here, and you're the same as him".

Then he has to lie on the bed and have blood taken for a variety of measurements: genetic tests, cholesterol and glucose levels, and more. Jo – who has an impressive collection of different-sized and colour-coded syringes – asks whether he writes with his right or left hand, so she can decide which arm to use. He replies, "I write with my right hand because I was made to when I was at school in Orkney. Otherwise I'm ambidextrous – but predominantly left-handed," and she is unsurprised and comments that the schools' insistence that pupils learn to write right-handed is fairly common within his Cohort.

While Jo is busy in her role as phlebotomist (a good word, we all agree) Eddie recounts an occasion when he and the team were sent to work on a lighthouse for several days. "The helicopter arrived with the tools and the food, but without a TV, and the others complained. I said to them, 'What do you want a TV for?' But the helicopter was sent back – it costs about £800 an hour – to fetch one."
So how did Eddie usually occupy his free time on the lighthouses? "I'd take my radio and my magazines."

At the end of the blood-letting, Eddie says he wants a gold star for making so little fuss!

After Jo has finished with him, and while Catherine is still occupied with another Cohort volunteer, we return to the waiting area for a cup of tea, and Eddie tells me that he retired from the NLB twelve years ago. He had loved his work and was very upset to have to leave; his colleagues gave him a good send-off party, and part of a flashing-light as a retirement present.

He has never lost his interest in engineering and, when I make the mistake of mentioning that my husband has a lathe for model engineering, is quick to offer back-copies of *Model Engineer*: "I've got a loft-full of them!" I just as quickly decline (it's only a few years since my husband was persuaded to part with his own collection.) That of course brings us back to the topic of hoarding: "If you google me you can find the piece I wrote about it." Unlike many of his age cohort, he is competent at using a computer and the internet: "I guddled around—" (we both agree that 'guddled' is another fine, expressive, word) "—and taught myself," he says.

One of his hobbies is an interest in narrow-gauge railways, and recently he took time to visit the restored railway at Alston in the Pennines, then stayed in Sedbergh and went down to Ravenglass on the Cumbrian coast to ride on 'La'al Ratty'.

There's quiet regret in his voice, although he is smiling, when he says, "I always wanted a bungalow with a loft so I could make my own model railway up there. People gave me model railways – I still have the Hornby ones in boxes – but it's too late now, I don't suppose I'll ever do it."

He was able to take that trip to Cumbria because his wife was briefly in respite care. For the past thirty years Norma has been suffering from Multiple Sclerosis, and Eddie explains that he arranged to have his Cohort testing done today because she is having two weeks' respite care at Liberton Hospital. "It's been a slow decline. She's in a wheelchair so there are limits where I'm able to take her. I very rarely go out now – but it doesn't bother me, there's plenty to do in the house and the garden."

Catherine is now ready for the final session of his testing. First are the two short stories, about which I have already heard a great deal; the aim is to test immediate memory and retention of information. She reads the stories at a measured pace, and repeats the second – all are read with exactly the same emphasis. Eddie has to remember as much detail, including the sequence of events and as many of the same words and phrases as possible, and repeat as much as he can after each reading. (He will be asked to recall the stories later, too, after a series of entirely unrelated tests.) I'm fascinated to discover how much he (and I, silently) can remember after each repetition, how the process of logical recall builds: small details come back, even now.

Then there are three tests for verbal fluency, each one minute long, when he is asked to think of and say aloud as many words as he can beginning with specified letters. ("What happened to 'light-house'?" I ask later. But I like his link between 'lichen' and 'liken')

The National Adult Reading Test (NART) and Wechsler Test of Adult Reading (WTAR) test vocabulary, and require him to read aloud from two lists of words. There are very few that he mispronounces, although he comments at the end that, "There were some words there I haven't stumbled upon in my travels through the world."

Letters and numbers to remember and sort, follow, and by 3.30pm I'm privately struggling as the combinations become progressively longer. Eddie is apologising more frequently, and hesitating, and suddenly capitulates: “Sorry, Catherine, my concentration is slipping. I know I can’t do any more.” He’s already been here for about four hours, but it’s not all over yet: for his final task, he is left alone to re-sit the original Moray House test that he took when he was eleven years old.

While he’s occupied, Catherine and I go into another room and talk about the testing process. I had been impressed from the start at the welcoming manner with which she set us at ease, and her unobtrusive patience and encouragement, carefully balancing praise with non-committal comments. It requires delicacy and skill to make a volunteer feel comfortable and unembarrassed – and to want to return, as many of the Cohort have done, several times.

Every part of the tests is carefully standardised, she explains, and the marking of results is double-checked, first by herself and then by another member of the team. She shows me how she might make explanatory notes next to certain results, to help the double-checker: for example, if a participant were deaf and had heard the letter B as a D. In addition, the cognitive testing team meet weekly on Mondays, to discuss any concerns they might have. “Ian [Deary] wants us to have top-quality data, hence the need for double-checking.”

This is important because the data are available to collaborators within the scientific community – and since other researchers can request data sets on different topics, all the data and results are anonymised, with each participant given an individual number.
While we wait for Eddie to finish his Moray House test, Catherine tells me that she was born in Kendal, and her

parents live there still, so she makes the journey to Cumbria quite often. She joined the *'Disconnected Mind'* team after graduating, but took time out to study for an MSc in Health Psychology at the University of Stirling, from which she recently graduated with Distinction. Like so many of the team, she says she loves meeting the Cohort study's participants – she now knows many of them quite well, having met them through two 'waves' of testing. "Sometimes they ask me, 'Isn't it boring, sitting in this room doing the same thing time after time?' But I love it – it varies every time, everybody is so different."

This enjoyment, and empathy with the 1921 and 1936 Cohort participants, is a strikingly common factor across members of the research teams.

At about 4.30pm Eddie Dishon's day of testing for the *'Disconnected Mind'* project on the LBC1936 is over – he has been there since 11am. As he leaves he is as ebullient and cheerful as he was in the morning, saying how much he has enjoyed the day. I have enjoyed it too, and we agree to meet up again so he can tell me about the "travels through the world" that cover the missing years in the narrative of his story.

'The missing years'

It's late March, one of those blue-skied, sunny days that startled everyone into believing that Spring, even Summer, had arrived: the following week, snow blasted the hills and streets. We meet for lunch at the White Lady Inn in Corstorphine and I am honoured that this time Eddie has

brought his wife, Norma, with him.
They have planned ahead, previously trying out the food and the wheel-chair access, and Norma is already waiting at the table in her motorised wheelchair when I arrive. She has silvery, shining hair, and a round, seemingly unlined face; her conversation and interjections throughout the lunch are gentle, and laughter is often in her voice.

Eddie gets us settled and goes to the bar to order food and drink. I remember his comment about being 'soft-hearted' about spiders: consideration and kindness seem to be part of his make-up (even if, as I discover later, he was a "bit of a wild man" when he was younger!). He is constantly, unfussily, solicitous of Norma's welfare throughout the meal.

While Eddie is up at the bar Norma confides that she's glad that he's "calmed down a bit, earlier he was very wound up". Apparently one of her two carers is new and young, and "all she wants to do is have a cup of tea and sit and chat." As well as dealing with this, Eddie had also been to the Western General that morning for his MRI scan for the Cohort study. I apologise for the extra disruption that our meeting must be causing, but she assures me how much he has been looking forward to our lunch. "And he's a workaholic, he can't sit still!"

When he returns to the table Eddie shows me some photos of various lighthouses; we look at Dubh Artach, and he explains that pillar rocks are rocky pinnacles often far separated from the mainland, so reachable only by sea or air. Our lunch is brought to the table, but he is keen to tell me more about his 'wanderings' while we eat.

Rolling Easter eggs down the roof of Bell Rock lighthouse, 1987

So we return to 1959, when he came back from National Service with the RAF in Northern Ireland, to rejoin Ferranti in Edinburgh as a mechanical engineer.
He worked there for another four years, he says; then, while drinking with his friends on a Sunday night, in their usual hotel, "one of us had this bright idea. 'We're always doing this every Sunday, how about a change?' It seemed a good idea, we talked about what we should do, and then someone said 'Let's emigrate!' " By the end of the evening they had decided on Australia and, "The very next day – it was April 1st – we all went up to Australia House and started it off, for better or worse."
They – one electrical and two mechanical engineers – left in November on the £10 assisted passage, to work at Broken Hill Proprietory (BHP), Adelaide, a company founded on the mining of silver and zinc. The jobs fell through, so they went instead to a steel works in Newcastle, New South Wales. During their stay in a migrants' hostel, they "caused some disruption and were encouraged to look for alternative accommodation". Eddie found a flat for the three of them near the beach. "We were never off it. Even when we should have been at work. Sunbathing, in and out of the water, a little drink ... Eventually we'd say, 'Whose turn is it to phone and say we're all sick?'."

He came back to Scotland for few months in 1966 for his brother's wedding, the homeward boat journey taking four

On board the Sitmar cruise liner "Fairstar" bound for Southampton from Sydney: 'First Sitting' - second Prize in the Fancy Dress competition, July 1966

weeks, the return taking three, each time sailing through the Suez Canal. On his return he asked for another job at BHP, but in view of Eddie's known record, "the boss said, 'No way!' "

So, Eddie tells me, he walked up the road to where there was a company that made wire rope. "They interviewed me and said they'd let me know. By the time I'd got back to the apartment there was a telegram waiting for me, saying 'Please come back, there's a job for you'."

In 1967, after the three years that were mandatory for the assisted passage, he came back to Edinburgh and Ferranti. Even though Eddie can't speak any German, *Wanderlust* clearly crept up on him on Sunday evenings. "I was working overtime one weekend, and someone had a Sunday paper and saw an ad for agency work in Germany. He was showing it round, 'Look at how much they're paying!'." So in January 1968 Eddie set off for Munich and joined Siemens in their machine shop for about a year. However, the agency couldn't or wouldn't get him a work permit and since he didn't want to be working illegally, he came home, to a job at Wireworks in Granton.

Norma had previously worked at Ferranti, which is where she and Eddie had originally met; they had been friends for a while: "I knew Eddie, and I thought he was lively and good fun," she says. Soon after he returned to Granton, they got together.

In 1972, six months after their son David was born, joining Norma's own children from a previous marriage – John and Susan, who were aged six and five respectively – a neighbour saw an advertisement for the Northern Lighthouse Board, and showed it to Norma's mother, saying "Eddie would like that". The NLB wanted artificers (engineers), especially people who could maintain diesel engines and generators and optics. "A friend asked me what I knew about lighthouses—" Eddie gives one of his big grins, "—and I said, 'Not a lot at the moment but I'll get a book out of the library'." He was given the job on a Thursday in June 1972 and told to go off to Orkney on the Monday. "They said, 'Just go – someone will be waiting for you there'."

Norma joins in: "We had David by then, and I said, 'If you're going away I think we should get married'. " They were eventually married in a Registry Office on March 13th 1973. "And, Eddie being Eddie, he said 'Well, that's that over, I can go and finish my crossword now'." Norma went off for a cup of tea with her friends and Eddie went back to work. "They asked me, 'Why are you all dressed up?' And I said, 'I just got married!'."

Norma is very calm and matter-of-fact about how she coped with the children when Eddie was away for such long periods: "Well, it wasn't difficult, that's what you did." When David started school she got a job nearby and could collect him at the end of the day. Her own two children have always treated Eddie as their real father, she says. "They say things like 'I must have got that from Dad' or 'I must take after Dad in this ..' even though it's not possible!"

Finally, I ask Eddie about something that has been puzzling me ever since I 'shadowed' him during his tests, relating to his short article about hoarding and his proficiency in reading the words in the NART and WTAR lists. At considerable risk of sounding patronising, I want to know how, if he left school at fourteen, he writes and reads so fluently.
He sits back in his chair, genuinely puzzled. "I don't know," he says, and pauses. "I've always been good at crosswords." Norma smiles and tells me, "He knows a lot. If anyone wants to know anything they always say 'We'll ask Ed.' And the children will phone up and say 'Does Dad know about such and such?'." She adds, "You always said that doing Latin helped, didn't you, Ed?", and we talk about learning Latin and English grammar.
"I like to use adverbs," Eddie suddenly says. "I like to fling them in. I'll talk about 'doing something correctly' rather than 'doing it right'." He has an amused frown for a while after that and I suspect he is going to think about this further.

The waitress comes to take away our plates, and Eddie hastily finishes his now-cold fish. Like all good *raconteurs*, he has enjoyed searching his memories and telling a story: he would like others of his generation from the NLB to tell their stories too, before the memories are lost.

There's a warmth and great *rapport* between him and Norma, but although they seem almost to know what each other is thinking, he surprises her just before we leave. They are laughing about the huge, barely possible, task of sorting through Eddie's hoards of unlabelled photos to find ones relevant to his story, when Eddie suddenly admits that he has already begun the process – and has "started putting some photos in a shoe-box."

February and March 2012

Professor Ian Deary
Director, CCACE

Ian Deary talking about the Mental Survey in front of a photo of Godfrey Thomson

"One of my weaknesses is I'm not a moaner – that's possibly a strategic error."

It's a good line, and makes us both laugh. We're in Ian Deary's office, a large room warmed by the autumnal colours of the trees in George Square, its open windows letting in the laughter and chatter of passing students. Ian is relaxed, leaning back in his chair, hands behind his head, sometimes staring into a corner as he thinks through his answer to a question, sometimes speaking quickly, looking at me to engage my attention, as he talks about his work and other enthusiasms. He is now sitting in one of the low chairs that are arranged invitingly for informal discussions, but very often, if one passes his open door, he is to be seen standing, working at a tall desk above which are fixed four computer screens. The open door is important – while we are talking a research student and one of the data analysts drop in, each bringing different pieces of information – and Ian clearly revels in the multitude of different interactions and ideas that each day brings, saying later, "I'm pretty good at handling things as they come along – a clean desk is the best way to come at things."

Ian Deary's medical and academic qualifications and his impressive and ever-increasing list of awards are all well-documented, in his University webpages, *Who's Who, Debrett's* and even *Wikipedia.* He is Professor of Differential Psychology at the University of Edinburgh and also, since 2008, the Director of the Medical Research Council Centre for Cognitive Ageing and Cognitive Epidemiology (CCACE), based in the Department of Psychology; today, though, as an initiator and leader of the Lothian Birth Cohort studies, he is talking about his own *Lifetime.*

Ian was born in May 1954 in Carluke, Lanarkshire. "It was a very countrified existence. I was almost never worried about going anywhere, the burn, the woods, the quarry with fossils in it ... fantastic to be able to wander around."
His father was a cobbler and saddler, and then a labourer, and the family was never well-off; from early on, Ian says, "I worked a lot, I've been working since I was eight. I managed to badger someone who had a grocer's van in Carluke to let me help, and I'd jump on the back of his van, and be going in and out of people's houses delivering their fruit and vegetables." He did this until he was seventeen years old, so "was self-sufficient in pocket-money from eight years on!"
He went to the local primary school where "we had mental ability tests, and depending on how you did, you could have the choice of different schools. Hamilton Academy—" his secondary school "—was the place you went to if you did well. It was odd going from a council-house background to a school where everybody was thinking of going to university."

While in his fifth year at the Academy, when he was seventeen, he decided to apply to Glasgow University to study medicine, but after only two terms of the course he had to give up because he "wasn't well off enough to keep going." Instead, he worked for five years in the Blood Transfusion Lab at Law Hospital and took day release and evening classes at Glasgow College of Technology where he gained an HNC (Glasgow Caledonian University, as it is now, presented him with an Alumni Achievement Award in 2009).

Ian at age 21 on the banks of the Clyde near his home town of Carluke

But medicine was still what he really wanted to do, and he came to Edinburgh to enrol as a medical student: "Coming to it later was good, I was more mature, I knew what the world of work was like." In the middle of working towards his degree he took an intercalated course in Psychology, and, "I discovered psychology! After that it was a case of finding a way back to it when I'd graduated. Psychology runs through me."

Two house jobs in Edinburgh hospitals followed, after which he moved to the Maudsley and Bethlehem Hospitals in London to practise Psychiatry. But then, only two years after he had graduated in Medicine, a lectureship came up in Psychology in Edinburgh, and he was soon not only a lecturer but also a postgraduate student working towards his PhD.

Having also, during this period, studied for and taken his professional exams in Psychiatry, "it became a decision between research in psychology or practising psychiatry. There was a very intense period when I was busy with my job in Psychology, was sitting my psychiatry exams, and was writing up my PhD. By then I had three young children, and was warden in a hall of residence."

He and his wife Ann had married in 1978, and their first child was born in 1979. "It was the best thing we ever did," Ian says. "Having children when you're young means you have the energy to enjoy them. And you're still young when you have grandchildren." They had their three children while "doing two stints of three years each in a hall of residence. It was at the back of Arthur's Seat, with safe gardens. It worked out fine, the children had a wonderful time – the ambience of having students around creates such a nice atmosphere."

Their two now-married daughters are both teachers locally, and their son studies painting conservation in Newcastle; as a family they are close. "On Fridays, we all meet and eat in one of our houses and tell each other about our week," Ian says and, on the rare occasions when he can be persuaded to take a holiday, "We sometimes rent a big cottage with all the family. The boys do the cooking. It's absolutely harmonious, we get on very well."

They now also have a grand-daughter and although she's still too young to do any serious walking, Ian and his son and his father have done several "three generations walks" together, along the Great Glen Way, St Cuthbert's Trail and the West Highland Way – "my Dad is eighty-two, but there are many gardens in Carluke that he looks after, and he still always walks there, carrying his tools."

Ian's parents had only a basic education, but this in no way limited his mother's interests. "The most memorable influence from my whole childhood was my Mum. She started oil-painting, she started interests in all kinds of things... She took a bus to London to the Tutankhamun exhibition! Nobody would have thought of that, nobody in our circle was doing anything like that. She encouraged our artistic and cultural interests. She took us to the theatre." There was the Home Service (as it was then) on the radio, and BBC2. "There was lots of music around, she always played music – I can remember even before I was five years old, hearing 78s of rock and roll."

Ian playing a saxophone solo at a Dancing Mice gig

That had an influence that lasts even now. Ian played in various bands in his late teens. He admits, "I did pick up a guitar and teach myself how to play it." But then his father bought him a "beautiful brass and plastic alto sax. When I sold it later and bought a soprano sax, I realised I hadn't known how special it was." He took some classical training in playing the saxophone for a year, but by the time he was a student he was playing in a punk band called *The Government.* And at medical school he also worked as a music journalist for '*Sounds*' magazine – "I got £30 per thousand words. It was quite handy money when surviving on a student grant – my wife wasn't working, and by then we had a baby."

Then, in 1989, he and three friends formed the band, *Dancing Mice.*, in which Ian is song-writer, singer and saxophonist. "We meet every Wednesday evening for the 'three Rs' – to record, write, rehearse." To date they've played between thirty and forty gigs, and have produced five albums: about a hundred people came to the launch of their recent album, *13 Difficult Lessons.*
It must be rather different from his departmental work? Surprisingly, Ian disagrees: "It's not unlike the job here – we have deadlines to meet, and I've got standards, and three tough referees to get past. I try to write good melodies with good lyrics." He smiles when he says, "I'm lucky to play with people who can play well, I'm not very talented myself."

"Why do people give up exploring new types of music? I listen to Radio 6 Music a lot, and I like hearing new bands and interacting with a circle of young folks." He laughs. "But it's difficult to find people to drag along. My wife's not keen!"

This interaction with 'young folks' is an important stimulus – "Students keep you thinking, breaking down your preconceptions" – and clearly has also created within him a strong sense of responsibility towards them; the theme of responsibility surfaces several times during the afternoon in different contexts. Later, when asked about special moments during his job, Ian pauses for quite a long time, staring at the ceiling before saying, "When there are nice things that happen to other people – when the PhD students pass their viva, or a good paper gets published. You know what I mean? When we were all together, to see whether our paper had been accepted for 'Nature', I got one of them to click on the button – and then we had a group hug, it was so special."

The research too is special. At the start of the Cohort studies there were just three people in Psychology – Alison Pattie, Martha Whiteman and Ian – but the team has expanded and become a Centre, almost a department. Building the team, seeing how they work together, and how they form spontaneous friendships has given Ian lots of pleasure, "But I take it as a serious duty to find funding for the young people and allow them to go further. I've got the responsibility of keeping attentive to their needs and what they do, and getting the infrastructure to do it."

"Since the late 1990s when the study started, we've had to find funding *every* time we wanted to move on, we've had no core funding, unlike other British Cohort studies. The serious side is that one knows the continual effort has been worthwhile – nobody owes us a living."

It isn't just increased funding that has helped the expansion; the team has grown in other ways too. Ian shows me a print-out, a photo taken from the Department's mezzanine, looking down at a large group of young adults, who are all laughing up at the photographer and holding children and babies; Ian sits smiling in the centre with his grand-daughter on his knee, a youthful-looking patriarch. "In a speech recently I was talking about how the research team had grown – and last week they all got together and sprung this surprise on me. ..." He is obviously touched, and amused.

We return to the exploration of new ideas and experiences, a subject that has already been touched on several times, either in relation to other people – "When I was a Director of Studies, I wanted the students to get as full an experience as possible. University should be a broadening experience" – or

to himself.
There is poetry, for example: Ian was President of the University of Edinburgh Poetry Society (he tells me that Ian Rankin held the same post after him); he wrote poetry too, and their three-man writing group *The Linesmen* played in the Fringe in 1978 and '79: "We were compared favourably with Patti Smith!". And there is Art: "Lots of my friends were in the Arts. I had lectures and practicals for my medical degree during the day, and worked in the evenings, but I realised there was a gap before dinner, so I went to extra classes then – Philosophy of Science, History of Art ..." So, instead of hurrying round a gallery trying to look at all the pictures, Ian "was bowled over by the fact that one could be kept looking at one painting for an hour."

As for reading, he set up a Reading Group in 1998, for which the members have read more than a hundred and fifty books. As an illustration of how he likes to find out everything about a subject, and follow it through, he tells me how he once bought Apsley Cherry-Garrard's book, *The Worst Journey in the World*, by chance – and became so fascinated with Antarctic exploration that he had to read all the biographies and accounts associated with the continent. But trying to read Wittgenstein when he was eighteen had been a mistake ...

Now he runs a Listening Group (it's a relief to find it has nothing to do with the psychiatrist's chair). "We choose four pieces of music on a single theme, and talk about how they're related." He listens to Shakespeare, too. "His language makes you work, you have to think about it, it's good mental stimulation. It's a shame that people don't think about how short life is, and try to make it as pleasurable as they can."

And there's the cycling, although not quite in Wiggins' mode. He used to cycle to his medical jobs, and in the early days of the Cohort studies, he and Lawrence Whalley cycled at weekends. "I'd plan the routes, thirty to fifty miles long, to the Borders, or Fife, or the Four Abbeys. We'd talk as we cycled. And we'd look for where there were charity events – I remember the Cat Rescue Ladies in Innerleithen, we had the best slap-up tea and cakes there, it set us up for the rest of the ride!"

Three generations: son-in-law Iain, Ian, father Hugh, and son Matthew at the end of their four-day St Cuthbert's Way walk (2009).

There is a bike behind the office door: he still cycles to work.

Does Ian think that he is 'driven'? His conversation, until now a mixture of laughter, seriousness and self-deprecation suddenly stops. There is a surprisingly long pause while he thinks about his answer, and then he asks,
"Driven – or drawn? I think I'm *drawn* – to the interesting things."

While he has been talking about the many avenues he has explored, an image had been growing in my mind, a cartoon depiction of an explosion, a bubble with *'bam!'* in the centre; and now I see that the bright rays are shooting out in all directions – towards different targets.

The Cohort Studies

"Counting leaves in trees is useful
And provides the shade where you can hide
From the roots and build the picture
See the whole from out and then inside"
(from 'Agenda for Change', in 'Improbable Popular Songs': copyright Ian Deary 2012)

"My life is split into two periods – Before and After the Scottish Mental Surveys. I remember when my friend and collaborator Lawrence Whalley and I came across the archives – it was a joint 'stumbling across' – and Lawrence claims I said, 'This will change our lives'."

Hanging on the wall of Ian's office is a painting of a man's head in profile, a man with a thoughtful, lined face, and a kindly expression: Godfrey Thomson. It was Thomson who devised the Moray House intelligence tests that the Cohort members sat when they were eleven years old, and it is the archived results of these tests that have formed the basis of the Cohort studies.

Ian says he has come to appreciate Thomson's psychology and how his life's mission was that people's talents should be appreciated. "Without making too strong a point of it, sometimes I see parallels in my life with that of Thomson, and his love of what he's doing, *communicating* what he's doing, and his desire for everyone to have equal and fair education, supported by the state."

IQ tests were thought by Thomson to be "the least bad" method of doing that. "I've always been fascinated by the idea of why people used these IQ tests – they were from a different world, where few people had more than a few years

of secondary education. I do think I've been paid to do my hobby for the last twenty years. Not a day goes by without thinking that."
"I see the work we're doing now as making proper use of the Scottish Mental Surveys and the Cohorts, looking at how people age and how their lives work out. Also, I have come to think that it is important to understand about Godfrey Thomson's work, and why it has been forgotten."

(This other story, of Godfrey Thomson, and how Ian saved so many of Thomson's papers and manuscripts a mere twenty-four hours before Thomson's house was emptied and then demolished soon after, is a fascinating tale of serendipity and a dash through the city on a bike; a brief account can be found in the *History of Psychology*, 2010 *, and it's a story that should be told again elsewhere.)

I mention that in my conversations with LBC participants, several have been pleased and very impressed by the way they are treated as 'special'.
"They are. It's a great human story – and what gladdens my heart is how much people selflessly contributed their time, back when these surveys were done. It was done on a shoe-string, and used lots and lots of time. And to think that those children have come back and are helping us after all these years is amazing. The individuals who have come back – *factually* they are special, that's the truth; there aren't any other Cohort groups that have that.
And like all good stories, this one is especially good because it has history and a poignancy."

* History of Psychology, 2010, vol.13, pp95-100. *Archival sources for Sir Godfrey Hilton Thomson*. Ian Deary *et al.*

Reverend Elspeth Dougall

LBC1936

Elspeth Dougall has been thinking about Moses and the Burning Bush. Although she has retired from full-time work as a Minister in the Church of Scotland, she still takes the occasional service – and this means writing a sermon for next Sunday. "I cannot cope with deadlines, I have to start thinking about the sermon on the Monday morning rather than do it in a last-minute rush," she smiles, leaning forward in emphasis.

Late-autumn sun is warming the room, brightening the chrysanthemums in a vase on the hearth. We are in the first-floor living-room of the house that she and her late husband Ian bought twenty years ago, a comfortable room that serves as both sitting-room and dining-room, separated from the kitchen area by a low peninsula of cupboards. The apartment occupies one-third of a large stone-built Victorian villa in the Newington district of Edinburgh, and as she brought me upstairs Elspeth had speculated that it might formerly have been the servants' quarters. Outside, the red berries of a cotoneaster tree gleam in the sun, as yet untouched by the blackbirds.

But we are talking about sermon-writing: "There's that awful stage where you have no ideas, they're not flowing. Then there's the creative stage when it's all happening, when it's exciting. And then ... the interaction, and the *life* of taking a service."

I ask the question that writers are so often asked by their au-

Elspeth in Malaga

diences – where do the ideas come from? "The ideas come from things that you're reading, picking stuff out of the ether – your mind's collecting ideas. Perhaps something you've completely forgotten comes back out of the blue."

This sounds just like the process of writing short stories, and half-jokingly I suggest that Elspeth should try this, but she laughs and says she doesn't have that kind of imagination.

Elspeth Dougall was ordained as a Minister of the Church in Kenya, in 1989. The desire to go into the Church was not the result of a mid-life epiphany: "From very young, perhaps the age of ten, I thought that was what I'd like to be. But it was pointed out to me that 'ladies cannot be Ministers' – so the idea got shelved." But even then, "my father always said I'd either go on the stage or in a pulpit."

She was born in Newport, across the river from Dundee, where her father was a jute-merchant and her mother was, before her marriage, a sewing-teacher. "We lived on the edge of the village, with the fields beyond. I'm one of those people who say 'When I was a child we used to play anywhere.' We were so lucky. I wandered around on my own a lot – I have memories of just *being* ... in the woods, in the fields. And I still get great pleasure in walking, just seeing, just looking ..."

After sitting her Highers she went on to St Andrew's University to read History and Political Economy, and recalls spending a lot of time singing, in the chapel choir and the madrigal group. She did social work for a year after she had graduated and then, in 1960, married Ian – and they went out to Kenya.

When they were on the boat out, they heard that the State of Emergency, brought in during the Mau-Mau uprising, had just been lifted. They lived in Kenya until 1972, first in Nyeri, to the North-West of Nairobi, and then at Kikuyu, and during this time Ian, who was already ordained as a Minister, spent his time teaching, initially lay-people, then later other Ministers.
Elspeth gave birth to their three sons while in Kenya, and throughout those twelve years they came home on furlough every 3 or 4 years. "Communication these days is so easy! In 12 years in Kenya I think we phoned home twice We sent cables, when a baby was born. Otherwise it was letters – if you wanted to ask your mother something, it would be two, even three, weeks before you got your answer."

On returning to Scotland, Ian worked as a school chaplain in Edinburgh and both of them were very involved with family and the local church.

And then, one day, about thirteen years later, "My husband came out with a bombshell! That he wanted to go back to Africa and he was going to drive there." Even now, Elspeth looks shocked, although she's half-laughing; she sits up and gestures with both hands. "I didn't want to. I didn't want to go back, I certainly didn't want to drive there! I'm not very adventurous. And I felt my life was just being thrown apart.

Everything was stirred up. But out of that turmoil came the space."

She stops and looks at me, then explains further: the structure of her life seemed to have crashed – but with that came "the space", which could now be filled with something she had always wanted to do, to become a Minister. "Actually I'd been thinking of it for thirty, even forty, years. And now the opportunity arose, and I thought '*Why not?*' I told Ian that this was what I wanted to do. And he said "Go for it!"
So, after thirty years' absence, she returned to University, this time in Edinburgh. "I found I loved it, I really enjoyed the study." As a mature student she was much more interested in the work than she had been as an 18-year-old, and in 1988 she graduated as a Bachelor of Divinity.

Her husband, meanwhile, had driven to Africa in his Land Rover with their oldest son and two others. Ian had been born in Kenya, and to drive there "was something he'd always wanted to do." It took him about ten weeks. Elspeth joined him a year later, in 1988, and she was ordained in Kenya in 1989 and appointed to a Girls' High School as chaplain and to teach Christian Religious Education.

"I have been very lucky – there were two things I wanted to do in life, one was to be a minister, the other was to be a mother who was at home for the children, as our mother was for us, and I have had the opportunity to do both."

"The first time we were in Kenya I was interacting with peasant women, some of whom had to carry all their firewood and water on their backs, as well as cultivating

Stuck in the Sahara desert; Elspeth and Ian, 1986

their small-holdings. As a European I was treated with a certain amount of deference. Quite unreasonably, of course. There was I living in a stone house with all the advantages of running water and electricity – most of the time! They were the ones with the real merit, incredibly hard-working and cheerful and full of joyful Christianity. The second time was different because now I was the same as everyone else. My face was one of only two white ones in the staff-room, but nobody noticed. My colleagues were educated African women, and I depended on their experience to guide me in my new role."

After their final return to Edinburgh in 1991, she spent ten years "in a job-share, almost unheard of for parish ministers at that time. I job-shared with someone who is another member of the LBC36 study."

In the late 1990s, Ian developed Parkinson's Disease. "But he didn't give in – he took his chance, he did things, he went off on his own. He went to Australia – he back-packed." Elspeth laughs. "Imagine, an elderly chap, with Parkinson's! He had a great time."

During that time, Elspeth was on a three-month sabbatical in palliative care, first at an Edinburgh hospice and then at St Christopher's Hospice, in London. "It was a very good experience, very useful – the hospice was a wonderfully

supportive place." She had 'digs' near the hospice and was also able to explore London. At St Christopher's she was working with the chaplain, observing, and visiting patients. "I was learning from all sorts of people in other disciplines too – social workers, occupational therapists. I learnt a lot about the different kinds of support they offered to patients."
Did patients question her, as a Minister, as to why this was happening to them? "No. It was more like listening – giving people the opportunity to speak, rather than giving them answers. There are no answers."

Apparently the chaplains were surprised that she didn't wear a dog-collar during her work in London. "There are two schools of thought: 'Oh, has somebody died?' The other is that, when people see you in a dog-collar, then they know who you are. It makes getting into hospitals easier! But many ministers don't wear dog-collars so much these days, only at services, or funerals, or a hospital visit."

Elspeth and her colleague retired from their parish in 2001. Afterwards she held a three-month *locum* post, followed by occasional "pulpit-supply", and every year since then she has been involved in the Religious Book Section of the mammoth Christian Aid Sale held in Edinburgh in May. For several years, too, she helped support overseas students who were doing post-graduate study in Edinburgh sponsored by the Church of Scotland.

Even in 2001, however, the progression of Ian's illness meant that he was needing more and more help.
"I had a huge list of things I was going to do when I retired, like taking classes in computing and art and language and I had a shot at most of them, but in these last few years Ian's

needs have been the priority and now – " (Ian died in April this year) " – I'm finding my way into what's new."

Her elder sister lives in Dundee, and her two surviving married sons and their children live not far away, in North Berwick and Elderslie. Over the summer she has also visited "a lot of friends situated in nice places like Aberfeldy and Hexham. I've appreciated having time to visit and explore"; the week before we meet she had spent a week in Mallorca.

Recently, too, she has taken up painting, in acrylics, and she shows me a painting of a wooden pier on Lake Coniston that is hanging on the wall by the stairs, and another – "I'm quite pleased with that one" – of Eigg and Rum that is pinned to the fridge door. "I get a lot of pleasure – and frustration! – out of it."

And of course there is the singing. "I've always loved it. I'm in the church choir and the Edinburgh Bach Choir." Earlier she had shown me a booklet of her letters and photos, from her Kenya days, that she had put together and printed out, and I'd commented on a black-and-white photo of her playing the piano to her two small boys. But she smiles and shakes her head, "I'm not an instrumentalist, though I can use a keyboard to learn my notes."

She uses a computer keyboard, too, and fetches a laptop from downstairs to show me some photos. The book of Kenya letters, some of which have been added to by Ian (his comments are in bold type) will be a fine memento for her family of those important years, and Elspeth hopes to get around to compiling another two or three. Meanwhile she's started to work on her Spanish again: "Sometimes I laugh and think, why am I doing this, worrying about remembering a Spanish word, when I can't even remember an English word?"

She is enjoying being part of the Cohort studies, and says that "Ian Deary makes you feel you're the most valuable people in the world." But, like many others, she finds the testing very hard work, requiring considerable concentration. The original Moray House test, which she has re-sat, was full of very difficult questions.
"They were like the problems we had to do in Arithmetic at school and I could never solve them. My father used to say 'Get rid of the red herrings and you'll see what the questions are about.' But I could never get rid of the red herrings!"

And yet she ended up doing what she had wanted to do since the age of ten. "I was never ambitious to get on – I just wanted to do pastoral work and lead worship. I was never looking to be a convenor of committees." Elspeth looks across at me and smiles; her lively face seems unlined, despite her age; her short white hair gleams, and there is a deal of seriousness behind her smile when she says, "I'm not a feminist. I didn't want to be a female Minister, I wanted to be a Minister. Have I ever had doubts? Yes, of course, and I still do, but I have always found God there when I needed Him most."

October 2012

Some points of view

Dr Martha Pollard, CCACE, January 2012:
"There's an interesting tension here between what is truly important in someone's life and what is expressed in data. The *essence* of the person is not there."

An LBC story-teller
"I enjoyed reading it, could not believe it was me I was reading about – it made me appreciate the good life I have had. I also read the other [stories], and about their lives – it was very interesting, hopefully we may all meet up sometime."

Dr Alan Gow, CCACE, January 2012
"People volunteer for different reasons. Some say, 'Why *wouldn't* you help?'. Others come because they get a good clinical work-up every 2½ -3 years, like an MOT. Others come out of scientific curiosity. Some because they have had someone in the family who had dementia, and they see this research as helping find out why memories decline.
"It's incredibly useful to me to see them in the face, in the flesh. Until you see the actual people you don't realise the variation ... It makes me look at their data differently..."

An LBC story-teller
"I am extremely proud to be part of the LBC 1936. The idea to draw on the experiences of members is a stroke of genius, lang may your lum reek."

An LBC story-teller
"I wonder why I so readily agreed to participate, because I

don't find it easy making my story so public -- but I think the general idea of personalising the stats of the participants is a good one. ... One son said it made him smile (which I reckon means it is recognisably me), so congratulations. I have been reading the other stories and am amazed ... at what varied and interesting stories they have to tell."